Tiller and the Pen

Contributors

Michael Badham

Marian Blue

Ray Bradley

Eton Churchill

Mary Lee Coe

Joan Connor

Richard Morris Dey

Gregory Fitz Gerald

Christine Kling

Mike Lipstock

Tamsen Merrill

Daniel Spurr

John Tucker

Ben Wilensky

Tiller and the Pen
A Collection of Sailors' Stories

Edited by John Ellsworth

Illustrated by Barry Rockwell

Eighth Moon Press
P.O. Box 492
Northport, NY 11768-0492

Published by Eighth Moon Press
P.O. Box 492
Northport, NY 11768-0492

Tiller and the pen: A collection of sailors' stories.

ISBN: 0-9642853-0-4 (pbk.)
Library of Congress Catalog Card Number: 94-90405

Manufactured in the United States of America
This book is printed on acid-free paper

First Edition 1994

99 98 97 96 95 94   10 9 8 7 6 5 4 3 2 1

Cover art by Barry Rockwell

© 1990 John Ellsworth

For my young sons,
Christopher Shao Jiang and
Nicholas Shao Ching,
who have recently begun to venture.

Acknowledgments

Thanks to the writer's who made this book possible, to Barry Rockwell for his artistic vision and skill, and to my wife, Elizabeth, who gave me steerageway when there was none.

Contents

Preface

A Tiller, a Pen, and a Destination

Both a tiller and a pen are tools of exploration, navigation, expression, and discovery: one via the waterways of the natural environment, the other via the waterways of one's mind, spirit, and experience. With a tiller or a pen, you may have a destination in mind or you may just start a passage of discovery, open-minded, ready to go where the elements of a situation or muse suggests.

I started this project with a direction in mind, but with a willingness to change course along the way, trying to be open to the suggestions of circumstance. The goal was to find short stories written by sailors for sailors. A call for yarns was first spoken in 1990. We asked that stories deal with sailing craft (pleasure or work) ranging in size and complexity from a sailing canoe to a brigantine. We were interested in a protagonist whose character unfolds during the story then reflects some change by the story's end. Stories were expected to be plausible, provide a strong theme which followed through, and be well crafted. With a few exceptions, the tales in this collection follow these guidelines.

This collection reflects the bindings of tradition, the power of observation, the mystery of myth and romance, rapport resulting from respect, the lure of the faraway and unattainable, and the quest for adventure, riches, and sustenance. These stories are the best from many.

Enjoy the passages. . . .

JOHN ELLSWORTH

Tiller and the Pen

Cutting Rope

by John Tucker

A young man sailing on a down-east schooner learns quickly about pride of possession, responsibility, and action.

YOU HAD TO HAVE a sailor's knife for cutting rope—Manila hemp it was in those days, sweet-smelling, the color of wheat. To cut it clean, you used the knife like a chisel, tapping it with a mallet. The blade had to be sharp, straight, and thick at the back. In the sailing books it looked like a little cutlass turned upside-down.

To find a sailor's knife my father took me to a store on Atlantic Avenue, near the fishermen's docks. Up two narrow flights

3

of stairs we climbed, hand-over-handing the big rope that ran through iron ring-bolts in the wall. At the top was a low-ceilinged room piled with boots and oilskins, hurricane lanterns, fog-horns, bins of hardware, anchors, compasses, cases of charts, and drums wound with chain, wire, and rope. At the back, in a glass display-case, there were jackknives, leather-handled knives from Sweden, and some with serrated edges for scaling fish, but not the knife I was looking for, the one with a rosewood grip riveted through a single piece of steel.

"You mean a rigging knife," said the clerk, taking out a folding model popular with yachtsmen. But I could have bought one of those anywhere. Sailors who carried them wore plain khaki trousers, and that wasn't my style at all.

"Suppose you're caught in a squall," I had argued recently at dinner-time. "Suppose the boat gets knocked down, and the halyards are jammed, and you have to cut the sail off. You don't want to be fishing around in your pocket. You want a knife on your belt, where you can get at it in a hurry." I had lifted this situation from a book on seamanship. I knew my father had cut his way out of some jams with nothing more authentic than an old Swiss Army knife, but he forbore to mention it, and I carried the day. Now he waited while I explained to the clerk exactly what was required. The clerk bent down to look in a box of odds-and-ends. Then he straightened up, and placed on the counter the knife of my dreams.

Douglas Fairbanks in *The Black Pirate* gets

driven up the rigging by enemy swords until there's nowhere left to go. Undismayed, he leaps out from the mast, slashing with his knife at the huge sail before him. He pierces it, and dangles there a moment; then, as it starts to tear, he angles his knife and rides the ripping canvas right down to the deck on the strength of his wrist. I loved that extravagant gesture.

I bought an oilstone and ground the blade several times a day. Oil and sweat gradually darkened the sheath to a deep mahogany; I began to wear it with the tip tucked into a back pocket.

At sixteen I went to Maine to crew on a schooner, a "windjammer" in the tourist trade. The *Martha* was a lot of vessel for a crew of four. Two hundred thirty tons and a hundred feet overall, she carried a two-hundred-pound anchor; her masts were like tree-trunks, too big to reach around. Hoisting her sails took six men, so when the passengers were indisposed, she didn't get under way until after lunch.

The captain was Frank Murray, a master mariner licensed to command vessels of any size in any ocean. He was eighty-two that summer, a short, round-shouldered man with eyes half-hidden by slanting folds of skin—they made him look like an old turtle. He had a raffle going every week, the prize a ship-model he'd made out of wood from the *U.S.S. Constitution*, so he claimed. The passengers didn't know he had a whole trunk full of the models, all the same. As cabin-boy, I made up his dank bunk and collected his empty bottles, but I wouldn't sell raffle-tickets. Not once that summer did he offer me a turn at the wheel.

One day we had a long, hard sail up a kind of fiord, a funnel of water between steep-sided hills. With the wind against us, we had to round a sharp bend, where there was very little room between the shore and a line of granite ledges. We tacked back and forth across the narrowing channel, but every time we turned, the big awkward schooner lost some of the distance gained on the previous crossing. Trying to make the most of every tack, Captain Frank would drive her in as close to the shore as he dared; then he'd spin the steering-wheel. At the same time, the mate on the foredeck would shove a small sail out against the wind—that helped to push the vessel's head around and bring her safely through the turn. I thought I could help out by doing the same with one of the bigger sails. The one I picked, however, had a lot of canvas in it, laced to a great boom that I could hardly budge. So I tied a length of rope to the boom, and while it was swung to one side of the vessel, I tied the free end of the rope to an iron ring in the deck. When the schooner began to turn, my rope held the foresail out against the wind, helping to bring us around. Then I jerked the slipknot out, letting the boom swing over, sauntered across, and tied my rope to a ring on the other side, ready for the next tack.

For a while, my invention did the trick—the schooner rounded more smartly on every turn.

Then the slipknot jammed. Frantically I yanked at the rope's end, but the weight of the boom and the wind-filled sail had settled on the knot. The schooner kept on turning, a sickening, slow-motion waltz that was taking her sideways towards the ledge.

"Cut it!" the mate was yelling. I stood there, frozen. Captain Frank left the wheel, the spokes turning lazily while he came up the deck, moving incredibly fast in his ratty cardigan with all the buttons gone but one, his bullet head forward, one hand groping in the pocket of his baggy pants.

"Look out," he said, and braced his feet. I dropped to a crouch and grabbed at the rail. His hand came up with a knife. I had a long time to look at it while he dug out the blade with a stubby thumbnail. It was a cheap penknife, its plastic handle decorated with a view of the Golden Gate Bridge and the words, "Souvenir of San Francisco." The blade might have been three inches long. All he did was touch it to the bar-taut rope and step back. The rope parted and the boom went over with a shivering crash that I thought would take the mast out of her. The terrible turning slowed, stopped. The *Martha* began to recover her course. Captain Frank looked at me.

"Don't do that again," he said.

*   *   *

In recent years I've moved a number of times, and always in the packing or unpacking I come

across my sailor's knife, mixed in with office supplies, or stashed in a box with chessmen and win-
dow-shade brackets. I'm glad it's there. The blade
could use a sharpening, and I still like the feel of the
rosewood handle.

Three Men and a Boat

by Eton Churchill

*Three generations experience a
contradictory, yet majestic sail one
afternoon on the family's 80-year
old family yacht.*

THE SMELL OF OAK in the last of the
winter fires is intoxicating; like an
aphrodisiac it arouses the deeper
memories of summer. Oak and cedar. That
summer smell is genetically imprinted for it
is the smell of the family yacht *LIZA*, a lean
and lovely relic which my great-grandfather
had built "down Maine." As a child I
learned *LIZA'S* oaken smell along with
Grampa's scent, a reeking wet wool odor
strong enough to simultaneously keep the

gulls curious and at bay. That's the way he was, too.

LIZA has had four captains in her eighty years, all of them bearing the same surname. I am the fourth in a direct line, my son Christopher will be the fifth if I can keep her going for another twenty years. I must. She is the queen of the fleet, the greyhound that still outperforms everything in the harbor and makes shutters click for miles around.

LIZA is lean and elegant on her mooring, her bows bobbing quietly to the soft seas building in the early afternoon breeze. My son Christopher, now ten, has been aboard all morning getting the brass and bronze bright for the afternoon sail. He has polished everything, and for no pay. It is expected: Silverado (as my father is known around the harbor) will be going out with us today. In his day he took home the silver, but today he is Captain Emeritus, and even young Christopher knows to be deferential to a former skipper who is not quite ready to relinquish the helm. After all, Silverado took LIZA to the Caribbean before it was fashionable to do so. He'll tell you about the Atlantic crossing too, if you ask. They only lost one man on that trip.

The breeze is up. The sky is a gauzy blue and the air a perfect summersoft. Gulls wheel above deck as if Grampa were still aboard in his wet wool sweater. The motion picks up a bit as the afternoon breeze excites the water. Christopher helps his grandfather hoist the mizzen. *LIZA* cocks into the wind.

With Christopher at the helm *LIZA* leaves the shelter of the harbor under power and slices into the brisk open bay. I'm at the main mast, spreading the balance of hardened canvas. Christopher and his grandfather wheel the ship off the wind, the sails fill, the cannonade of sail noise dies and *LIZA* leaps ahead. Silverado cuts the engine and the three of us delight in the moment as the old gal dances into the sparkling seas happy to be alive.

The moment is short-lived for Christopher soon reports a very stiff helm. I myself know the boat is not up to par—she seems loggy. Silverado offers to relieve Christopher who is all too ready to be elsewhere. He knows what has happened—we have snagged the line of a fisherman's pot buoy. Silverado soon recognizes the symptoms.

"Christopher, get that buck knife I gave you. We need to cut the buoy," he barks to the boy who is already headed below.

"We don't cut buoys anymore," I say, getting the boathook ready and starting the engine so I can reverse the prop.

"Why the hell not?" my father asks.

"Because that pot buoy is somebody's livelihood," Christopher says firmly. Respectfully.

"Bring her into the wind," I say to my father.

"You take the helm, skipper," he says. "I don't see why one pot buoy has to be saved. You've got to learn, Chris—everything you do on board is for the good of the ship. If a pot buoy puts the ship in peril, you cut it. Bad luck for the lobsterman."

"We don't cut buoys anymore, Dad. We're not in peril."

"You're raising the boy to be a sissy sailor."

Christopher and I manage to disentangle the fisherman's buoy

"It's Peter's buoy," Christopher says referring to his friend and mentor whose family has fished these waters for generations.

I take the helm and drive the old gal hard hoping the sprightly sail will clear the air of familial tension.

"God, she really does move, doesn't she?" Silverado says.

"Take the helm, Dad" I say as we approach a narrow passage between Robinson rock and Mark Island. We will have to beat our way through, a small exercise my father delights in, for *LIZA* is very quick on her feet. Christopher and I man the winches. Two other boats work their way through the little passage. Being first is not just a thought in Silverado's mind—it's a genetic necessity.

The first two tacks are elegant—we gain on the more recent plastic boats. The third tack is only mediocre as Christopher has some difficulty getting the jib in—he's not quite strong enough. For the fourth tack dad brings the boat perilously close to the rocks where seals bask in the falling tide. Christopher loves the seals—loves watching them—being close to them. I suspect sailing to him is just a chance to see the seals.

Silverado puts the helm over without notice. The jib backfills making it all but impossible for Christopher to release it. *LIZA* stalls in the wind and bobs near the rocks. In a moment I am able to release the jib and the boat comes 'round. We lose ground to the other boats.

"We should a had 'em," Silverado punishes.

"Sorry," Christopher says. The lust of the day is gone from him.

"Here, Chris, you take the helm. Your dad and I will handle the sheets."

"I'm okay here," Christopher says.

"Ready 'bout—hard over!" barks the helmsman. *LIZA* comes around slickly and we gain on the other two boats.

"Do you think we can blanket them—think we can beat them to the bell, Chris?"

"I guess," the boy says.

"Well, let's DO IT. READY 'BOUT—HARD OVER—GET THAT JIB IN. NOW! I SAY NOW! . . . GOOD . . . ."

The boy grinds the big winch for all he's worth. The jib snaps to, *LIZA* leaps ahead making a wind shadow for the other boats.

My father drives the boat relentlessly toward the rocks trying again to avoid a tack. He has done this maneuver thousands of times, always with the help of a good crew. Christopher and I have

Tiller and the Pen

surmised that Silverado knows these rocks as well as any seal. Christopher learns the meaning of "local knowledge" as the old wooden hull grazes the seaweed on the rocks. A foul up could mean an unstately end for *LIZA,* one of Christopher's important summer friends whose bronze he polishes without complaint.

"NOW!"

The helm goes over, Christopher releases, the sail crosses over and snaps to. We dart in front of the other boats forcing them to tack.

"Well done, mates—well done!" my dad says and waves pleasantly to the other boats as we move ahead.

"Remember this day, Christopher. Remember that this eighty-year old boat can whip the stitching out of those Clorox bottles with all their gadgets. And she'll take you across the Atlantic, too—something that Tupperware would never do."

Christopher smiles at me with the look that asks if Dad delivered the line with the same passion as he has on every sail through this small passage.

"That's enough excitement for the day," Dad says, giving me the helm and taking a position of repose in the cockpit, right next to his beer.

Soon we are on a reach along the backside of the island. The sailing and the seas are easier, yet the boat moves with equal speed. This is my tack—easy, fast, making the mark. Christopher is forward now watching the dolphins play in the bow wave. The "cottages" slide past us—all those blue blood names from Philadelphia and New York and of course Boston. What an effort to keep those summer traditions going! And the cost—my God how it costs to have one of those "wind castles" as the natives call them. Every year one falls victim to finances and becomes a B&B or a school or a reminder of the effects of fire.

And what about *LIZA?* Isn't maintaining an eighty-year old boat a bit of an indulgence? Probably. She is a thing, this boat whose seams are caulked with sentiment. She still has Grampa's odor, Dad's silver trophies, Christopher's polished bronze. Someday someone in the family will have to let her go. The tradition will end. I don't think it will be me or Christopher though.

Going home the wind is at our back. The boat is stable, the sun warmer, the harbor bobbing over the bow. This is Christopher's tack—sleepy, dreamy, slow. He takes the helm and lays back to look at the sky. He can steer by the feel. Silverado is asleep.

*   *   *

I feel like a nap as I sit before the last of the winter fires and smell the oak burning. Silverado's ashes were scattered in Robinson Rock passage last summer. He's gone. There are no more captains emeriti. *LIZA* is all mine now, with all her history, all her tradition, all her smells. Christopher and I will take her out—just the two of us for now.

Standing Watch

by Marian Blue

A retired mariner becomes entranced by a young lady sailor as she anchors in his harbor for an evening.

S HE RODE THE WIND into his bay, rode a wind which lightened even as she neared the small beach two hundred feet below his sun room. She came about on her little sloop, then up into the dying breeze. The mainsail fluttered lightly as it dropped onto the boom. The jib flapped two broad ripples, one to port and one to starboard, before it fell to the foredeck. She stepped quickly and lightly forward, slid the anchor over the bow. A light splash he could see but not hear settled her like a snow goose which had come in for a landing, glided to a stop, flapped its wings once or twice and then folded in on itself in peace.

Though the vessel rested, she did not. He watched while she bagged the jib, covered the main, coiled lines, and checked her anchor to make sure it was set. Soon she disappeared below and returned to the cockpit at sunset with a plate of food and a drink. When he focused his telescope on the can he identified it as *Coca Cola*. He was pleased she was a good Captain, one who would not dull her senses while anchoring alone in his bay.

While the sky turned from orange to scarlet to dusky pink then gray, he watched the little sloop. The white deck gradually became one with the water. Eventually he could tell where she lay at anchor only by the bobbing light out the cabin window. He wished she would light an anchor light which would arc through the night with each roll of the boat. But he knew she wouldn't bother. The bay was a known anchorage, though rarely used this early in spring. She would lie in peace, in the dark.

He lit no lamps himself but sat in a dark as complete as hers, sat in his wheelchair by the useless telescope and waited for dawn. Once he thought about eating, or going for a drink, but he didn't want to disturb the layering of thoughts that he felt woven in their almost-meeting, their sharing of his bay. What if he left watch and at that moment she should light a light, or raise sail and leave in the dark? He would never know her leaving, never be sure what direction traveled this visitor come with the wind. He must stand watch, not let the good Captain below rest uneasy.

By first light his eyes burned, felt scratchy with each blink. But he had not left his watch and he was rewarded by a million pink winks of light on the water below. Even her boat was pink with a pink mast. When she came out of the cabin, she stretched, ran her fingers through hair tinted pink, then shook her head and hair free and easy as though to feel the sunrise down to her very scalp.

When she went below and then returned with a cup he could smell the coffee, taste it—sweet and strong—across his tongue. He felt a bitter rebellion at the back of his mouth; she would, he was sure, like her coffee stronger than he preferred.

By the time the sunrise had turned the world yellow, she already had the mainsail and jib ready to raise. Today's wind came across the mouth of the bay, and he knew she would use no motor. She would ride the wind away, as she had come. She hoisted sail, pulled up on the anchor, hauled it quickly inboard, then scrambled to the cockpit to tighten her sheets. The sails flapped once, twice, then filled, lifted the vessel to speed like the snow goose preparing for long flight. When she reached the mouth, the sloop had a bone in her teeth. She rounded Point Maddox, headed north toward Fillip Island, and was out of sight.

He rubbed his eyes, stretched his arms over

his head. Strangely he felt no desire to sleep or eat. He was remembering the creak and hum of the rigging, the chuckle of water as it made way for the bow, slid along the hull. He licked his lips and savored salt.

Coffee on the Watch

by Ben Wilensky

*Reflective thoughts on watch are
evoked by the power of the black
bean.*

I love black berries brazened by the
sun
Mangled into magic powders and set
aflame
I love my coffee on the morning watch
Black and bitter brewed as strong as you
can make it
Pulling on the breezes
Calm and powerful as the seas
As strong as you can take it

Tiller and the Pen

I love this liquid majesty
This panther in my throat
Its smell is raw and radical
Its taste is insurrectional
Provoking me to set my kings and queens
adrift

In shark infested waters
A herd of humpbacked whales
Blows rings around my boat
They blow and spout the one true God
The one true force without a face
And liberate my foolishness
The need to speak

No sinning here or devilish constructs
No formal wrangling with recalcitrant bulls
Only the tides and tricky devils to monitor
The marginal movements of going out
And the wondrous movements of coming in

As I sip my coffee and study the charts
The tents flutter
The pennants dance
The caravans push into the wind

Each wave's a hump
Each particle of foam is tribal memory
Rays of blinding light
Long lines of camel vans traverse the dunes
Rising Falling
There before me: The crescent moon.

•

Coffee

on

the

Watch

Aground

by Joan Connor

A fisherman's visit ashore after
running aground produces a choice
he remembers for life.

C OME IN," she says without raising
her eyes, as if she'd been expecting
him. "Hang your oilskins on the
peg inside the door."

"Thank you." He peers into the dim
room. The cabin smells slick, oily with fish
and kerosene. Did she watch him run the
trawler aground, he wonders. Had she
watched him setting the anchor, rowing the
dinghy ashore? He cannot see the woman's
face. She leans over the counter, hidden by
a curtain of hair, her arm working a

cleaver—chop, chop, chop—across the damage board.

"Leave your boots," she says and points at the bench by the door.

As she turns her head, she parts the drapes of gray hair, pulls them back over her shoulders and twists them together in a single hank, kinking it into a loose knot at the nape of her neck. Even in this sulky light, she looks old. Age has bunched her features. Pouches of skin droop from her lower eyelids. Her nose clumps into a ball. Her lips corrugate. He tries to picture her face when it was young, but the task vexes him. Even in his imagination, he cannot iron out all the wrinkles. She coughs, and he realizes he has stared at her too long.

He glances out the doorway, checks the breeze, his dinghy pulled high, secure on the rocks.

"Behind you. The bench," she says and bends back over the counter.

"Oh, yes." He sits and tries to pry off his right boot with the toe of his left, but it just slides off the heel, well-greased with clam-flat muck. He leans over to peel his boots off noting a row beneath him, neatly paired, running the length of the bench. Men's boots, the rubber surfaces crackled from disuse.

Chop, chop, chop. The cleaver hacks across the board. "You fish?" she asks.

"Yes. Just starting out." His right boot yields with a squoosh.

"All men fish sooner or later. My husband, too," she says, chopping, then adds, "I knew you'd go aground there. That sand bar extends further out at mid-tide than people guess. Chart's wrong on two counts. The length of the bar and the name of the island. Chart says, 'Mystic.' But it's 'Missed It,' missed the sand bar. But strange boats rarely do. You'll be all right. It's a coming tide. No ledge out there. Just sand. Soft sand."

"Yes. I was lucky—running aground on sand bottom." He shakes his head at his own stupidity. "This part of the bay's new to me. I usually fish north of here. And when I do cross here, I usually cross to the west. I lashed the steadying sail hard toward the shore. *Mistress*, that's my boat, is pretty forgiving. She should free up as the tide rises." He kicks off his left boot and slumps against the wall. The door is a blinding rectangle of light in the dark room. An oily steam seals the windows. He sniffs. Fish chowder. A pot hangs on a tripod above barely smouldering coals in the fireplace. He searches for small talk. "It's warm," he says. "Indian summer. But it's a fresh breeze out there. Twenty knots and gusty."

She doesn't answer. She scoops up the chunks on the cutting board, crosses to the hearth, carefully side-stepping a rolled pallet, and plops the fish into the suspended kettle.

"Mackerel?" he asks.

"Blues. If you're hungry, help yourself." She nods at a stack of bowls on the counter.

But he doesn't move. It's too hot for chowder. He mumbles, "Thanks," and scans the shimmer of water and sand for *Mistress*. He shifts on the rough bench. The sparsely furnished room—three rolled pallets, two rockers, a table, a large wardrobe, and some scattered straightback chairs—has been out-fitted for function rather than comfort. He won-ders when he can get under way; he tries to calcu-late the tide and figure whether he'll make his cove before nightfall.

The woman's cleaver cuts the silence.

"Plenty warm," he says again. "But it's a strong Sou-westerly out there today. A lot of chop."

The woman only nods.

"Your husband fishing?" He'd noticed no mooring near the island.

The woman shakes her head. "Dead." The cleaver crosses the board with blunt little thunks.

"Dead." He shifts on the bench, murmurs, "I'm sorry," then asks, "Lost at sea?" Under him, the flappy boots slouch against each other and gape.

"No. Just dead." Her voice admits no sorrow.

It's a hard life, he thinks. Scraggles of hair have worked free from her hasty bun. He cannot see her face, but he remembers its lumpiness. She was beaten perhaps. He has known lobstermen like that—rarely at home and, when home, drunk and, when drunk, cruel, their wives quiet and sullen as bruises. No one mourns these men when they die. He studies his feet, picks some lint from his rag wool socks. "You're alone then?" he asks.

"Alone," she repeats. Her voice whets to an edge sharper than the cleaver's. She slaps a fillet onto the board. The cleaver drops rhythmically.

"Yours the only house on the island?" He pokes his boots with his foot. They skid forward a few inches, glued together with mud.

She nods. "Only one." She plows the fish chunks to the edge of the board with the cleaver, slaps down another fillet.

"Chop, chop, chop." The sound startles him. Not the sound of the cleaver, but a voice. A soft voice. A girl's voice. Only then does he see her sitting on the stool in the corner, half-obscured by the opened door of the wardrobe.

"Chop, chop, chop." Her voice again. Her hand pushes the door aside.

How did he miss her, he wonders. She is the only brightness in the room. Shiny as a jigging lure.

The old woman taps her temple. "Don't mind her," she says. "She's simple."

But he minds her. He gawks. In the shadowy corner of this fish shack with its stingy light and dingy future, sits the most beautiful woman he has ever seen. She is younger than he by a few years, he guesses, perhaps sixteen. Even by this light, her hair, agleam, tumbles to her shoulders, not blonde but impossibly yellow like goldenrods. Her eyes appear gray; in brighter light they might prove blue. But her eyes hold nothing but their color. Expressionless, they consider him.

"Chop, chop, chop," her mouth says again— her perfect mouth, a mouth he cannot imagine saying, "no." Her skin, undisturbed by the motion of her mouth, glides fluidly. Her face unsettles him—something glimpsed through layers of blue and placid ice beneath which sluggish waters stir—a face of great calm, except it is beyond calm. It is empty.

Her dress is plain, a gray-blue cotton, and reaches almost to her crossed ankles. Her bare feet perch on the rung of the stool. The curl of her pink toes makes him think of small birds—chickadees, titmice. But she stretches long and slender beneath her dress. He can imagine the hollows just inside her hips, the taper of her waist, silky in his salt-chapped hands. He wants to turn away from her; he knows he should turn away from her, but he cannot. His eyes fix, strive to read some response in her face. But there is nothing there. And this he realizes is what transfixes him—that vacancy, the lack of guile in her eyes—offset by her beauty.

His hands yearn to stroke her imperturbable skin. His fingers long to snarl in her yellow, yellow hair, his teeth to bite the plump ring of her mouth. In her gray stare, his eyes swim.

Chop, chop, chop. Not her voice now, but the cleaver's. His neck strains as he turns away from the girl.

"She's not right in the head," the old woman says.

He squirms. He feels as if the old woman is staring at him, but her eyes remain lowered as she talks to the rhythmic accompaniment of the cleaver.

"Born slow. Not much point in sending her off-island to school. Can't even dress herself." The woman waggles her head slowly from side to side.

He pictures the old woman dressing her, and he has to shut his eyes to keep from trembling at the image of the yellow-haired girl, pearly and naked.

"Her father named her Lily. I never much liked the name. Lee, I call her. It hardly matters. She doesn't answer to names. She doesn't really talk even. Just repeats sounds. So I call my daughter Lee."

He startles at the word "daughter." What magic tricks could time perform that would make this aged woman the mother of this girl? Or had the hardness of this woman's life prematurely aged her? "How did you lose her father?" he asks.

The old woman blurts a short laugh at the question. The laugh rasps, the laugh of someone unaccustomed to laughing. She coughs, recovers. "We didn't lose him." She stresses "lose," shaking her head.

"Chop, chop, chop," says the girl.

He turns toward her voice. Her beauty jolts him. He breathes hard as if he's been thumped on the chest.

Observing the senseless motion of her mouth,

his eyes slide down her hair, her shoulders, her arms to the small hands nesting in her lap. Incapable of resistance, he thinks. Fingers as delicate as twigs, fine as straws. Only then does he notice that the joint of her little finger is missing. The finger stubs, blunt just above the knuckle. He thinks of the sweetness of dark rum undercut by the sourness of lemon, the off-note that reminds you that you have an ear for melody.

"Chop, chop, chop." The meaningless words sound like an invitation, a chant. "Chop," she repeats, "chop."

He rises slowly, pulled by her voice. Forgetting the old woman, he crosses to the girl. He takes her hand, rubs his thumb over the shiny skin of her stumpy finger. He inhales the close lemony tang of her hair. He places his hand under her chin, tilts her head back and stares into the upturned face. He lifts her hair, brushes it back over her shoulders. He feels as if he has been fishing a long time. He cannot remember when he last had a woman. Perhaps many years. Perhaps never. He leans over her, lifting her torso toward him.

One chop stops him. The sound travels along his spine. He pivots. The cleaver stands on its own, its tip buried in the cutting board.

"Tide's coming. It comes fast when it comes there in the gut," the woman says. The cabin broods, still and airless. "You should be free now," she adds. She yanks the cleaver from the board and holds it.

His skin shrivels. The hair on his forearms bristles in animal reflex, tiny antennae transmitting danger signals. The woman says nothing, but his breath catches on something close to intuition or alarm. The cleaver glints with sharp intelligence, suddenly the most sensate, most conscious presence in the room—keener, more brilliant than yellow hair. Without looking at the girl, he releases her. He feels her weight shift from him as she settles onto the stool.

Time attenuates. A season has turned since the woman last spoke, but he knows only a minute has elapsed. His jaw works woodenly. "Yes. I should get my boots on and get back to the boat." Watching him, the cleaver gradually lowers itself to the board, lies down on its side.

But he does not turn his back to the blade. He eyes it intermittently as he pulls on his boots. He consciously averts his eyes from the girl, checks *Mistress'* lie. She's vectored toward deep water, headed up. He stamps his heels. Dry cakes of mud drop from the boots, puff small silty clouds as they land on the floor. He inhales slowly, self-consciously. The history breeding in the oil smells and fish smells of this dark, sad room rises, surfacing like a body lost at sea. Preternaturally alert, he sees the father, drunk, forcing himself against the girl, threatening his wife that he will kill their child if she interferes. She tries to force herself between her daughter and her husband. And her husband, who is a man who keeps his word, chops off the child's fingertip as a caution to her. Chop. The child screams. The woman waits, endures. When he is done, he passes out on the pallet. She binds the child's finger, listens until sleep mutes the girl's whimpering. While the child sleeps, the cleaver kills him.

The story loops through his mind. He doesn't know why he suddenly knows this story, but he doesn't doubt it. The knowledge is simply there like the first preliterate knowledge: breathe, suck.

He slaps on his oilskins and stands in the door frame. "Yup, she's floating free. Thank you," he says. But he barely looks behind him at his boat. As he leaves, he never shifts his vision from the cleaver

Wordlessly, the woman slaps another fillet onto the board. As he walks down the bank, he hears the chop, chop, chop diminishing behind him.

* * *

But sometimes in the shuttered darkness of his dreams, the sound grows louder, closer like his heart. He keeps time as it beats, chop, chop, chop, with a yellow-haired girl who sits on a stool. He is an old man now. But she does not age. Behind her cabin is an unmarked grave. He knows this although he never returned to the island misnamed "Mystic."

He might have earned himself such a grave. He once thought that on that day he'd made an easy choice of life over death, survival over lust. But as he's gotten older, the choices no longer seem distinct, either one, a desire to preserve his life. Either one could have affirmed him.

Had he been a different man, braver, perhaps, or crueler, he might have a memory now to warm him, a memory of lying with the beautiful girl who burns her way nightly into his dreams, a memory cleaving his heart. But he was not that man.

Sometimes he considers her father. How could a man commit such an act? He shudders with age and awe. No answer comes. Some hearts are uncharted. The yellow-haired girl comes and goes; his days and nights entwine, intermingle sleep and waking. They no longer separate into distinct states. Sea and shore. Sky and sea. When the dream ebbs, he lands. "Missed It." Again he runs aground.

The Sea Has Many Voices

by Gregory Fitz Gerald

"One touch of nature
makes the whole world kin."
—Shakespeare

SCUDDING NORTHWARD from the Virgin Islands to the July rendezvous of tall ships in New York Harbor, the windjammer *Liberty* couldn't dodge the sudden midnight rain squall. All twenty-two hands jumped to, began to shorten sail. A trainee, having just reefed the gaff-rigged trysail, lost his grip in a sudden wind shift and fell directly into the sea. In the blinding rain and turmoil, no one saw him fall. By the time his mates noticed his absence, he was already far astern.

41

Tiller and the Pen

Arms flailing, the trainee bobbed up in *Liberty's* wake coughing, gasping for breath, spitting out gouts of phlegm and sea, but otherwise unhurt. The *Liberty* yawed, vanished behind a thick sheet of rain. Floating in the dark, he repeatedly shouted for help as he heard his mates' responding cries diminish into sounds of just sea and rain.

Although the rain soon stopped, and the sky cleared, there was no sign of the *Liberty* anywhere. He understood aloneness as never before.

Struggling out of his ducks, the big man kept only his underwear and the belt with his sheath knife. He stared up at the clear, star-filled sky, breathing deeply, not through large, flaring nostrils but through his wide-lipped mouth— before he saw the red light, heard the bell toll above the sea sounds. More than a mile to port a combination buoy, with bell and flashing red light, rose and fell in the swells like a star fragment floating in an alien void.

He swam carefully, slowly toward the clanging bell, its light flashing redly: two short, one long; two short, one long—over and over again. Including several intervals of floating, more than an hour-and-a-half passed before he reached the buoy. For another fifteen minutes he clung panting to one of its lifting eyes. The rapidly blinking light made its slow crimson arc some seventeen feet above his head, and the bell rattled loudly, so close to his ears.

At last he heaved and wriggled his fullback's frame up the side of the swaying, guano-encrusted buoy; glass-sharp barnacle shells sliced into his flesh, blood oozing onto the pitted steel to be smeared, finally washed away by sea-spray.

The nearly naked man lay face down across the steel plates, salt water seeping from his skull cap of tight black curls, feet dangling close above the sea. For twenty minutes, panting, bleeding gently, teeth clicking, he sprawled just under the tolling bell, until at last he hauled his more than two hundred pounds erect and gazed about his tiny island.

The western sky glowed with the promise of a great city; coastal lights flickered on the horizon, but close by he could see nothing but an occasional phosphorescent white cap on dark water. At regular slow intervals a long finger of white light swept across the sky, leaving behind an even deeper blackness into which the quick flashes of red light gleamed but feebly.

To the rhythm of the bell he scooped handfuls of sea to stanch the bloody barnacle scratches. While leaning over the edge of his islet, the castaway could see a shimmering patch of the lightest pink—almost white even in that crimson light—beneath his buoy. For a long time he watched it undulate, pinkly phosphorescent far beneath the surface. He shuddered, gooseflesh erupting in the night breeze. Again he peered down at the thing, but it provided no explanations.

The bell allowed him little reverie—clanging and rattling so close to his ears, dominating all.

•

**Gregory
Fitz Gerald**

Quickly he removed his underpants, cut them into strips with his sheath knife, tied fast each of the four external clappers.

Quiet, broken only by soft sea sounds: a distant, diaphone foghorn intoned far to the northeast. A few pink-tinted wisps clung to the diminishing swell near his scarlet island.

Striving to remain awake, to keep watch, first he sat upright, but later gradually collapsed beneath his bell, one burly arm entwining a strut. Flashing two short, one long—the red light blinked on into the foggy, eyeless night.

The next morning a moist sun pushed slowly up above the fog bank, shone hazily through shaggy vapors clinging to the swells like random tufts of cotton wool. The castaway writhed, groaned, lifted his head, peered about, then pulled himself erect on his swaying islet. In the pale light his whole visible domain consisted of a few acres of sea and this metal cork bobbing about, bizarrely covered with red and black stripes that he knew signified the presence of a sunken obstruction.

A new and different sound had awakened him, but he could see nothing but his red light, flashing both night and day, and walls of fog. Now it came again: the prolonged deep bass of a ship's fog horn, different from the familiar diaphone sounding regularly throughout the night. The fog played such tricks he couldn't be certain from whence the signal came. He shouted, but in answer came only throaty blasts at two-minute intervals, steadily weakening until but a memory.

He settled down to wait for the fog to lift, washed himself—glad that the inflamed barnacle cuts had already scabbed. The inexplicable blob still wavered palely in the morning light, quivering shapelessly and as stark white as a dogfish's underbelly. Giant fish? A white metal drum? A submarine tumor of his buoy? A piece of submerged sail cloth? A sunken wreck? He knuckled his brown eyes, looked again. The blob didn't vanish; it only seemed to move gently back and forth.

When the fog began to lift, three sea gulls alighted above and lost no time in disputing possession—venting raucous rage upon this usurper.

His phobia for all fluttering creatures—birds and flying insects, anything with thrashing wings—sent him cowering, arms upflung before his face. The gulls circled his buoy in narrowing swoops, glaring, screaming imprecations from hooked beaks, soaring almost within arm's length. Their feathers, that from a distance seemed pure white, the castaway could clearly see were streaked grayly with filth. These sea fowls, with flickering wings, settled to wait on the steel ring surrounding the red lantern ten feet above his head. No sooner had they perched than the smallest discharged its excrement full upon the curly head of the castaway, who now filled the air with curses of impotent rage and disgust.

By midmorning the fog cleared. A dozen

times he chased the birds away, but they inevitably returned. From his swaying perch, captured only temporarily from the angry, wheeling birds, he stared longingly at the clearly visible, yet distant coastline.

"Too far," he said aloud. "Much too far. 'Now would I give a thousand furlongs of sea for an acre of barren ground.' That's what the man said . . . Shoo! Damn you!"

When he climbed down, the trio resumed their vigil with hungry eyes.

Just after noon a transoceanic flight buzzed overhead; he waved energetically but futilely. At mid-afternoon a dragger foamed four miles to the north trailing an entourage of seafowls his gulls promptly joined. Later, at dusk, dance music floated over a calmer sea from a brilliantly lit cruise ship three miles north. No one aboard heard his shouts.

He listened to his growling, empty stomach, watching the enigmatic white blob turn pink in the reddening light of nightfall, until he noticed clusters of sea snails, called periwinkles, clinging to the buoy below the waterline. Prying them free with his sheath knife, he sucked the periwinkles raw from their shells, followed them with a salad of algae hanging thickly below, washed it down with palmfuls of sea water and grinned.

* * *

During the clearer morning of the next day, his second on the buoy, still ravenous, the castaway overcame his revulsion for beating wings and tried to capture one of his sentinel gulls. They

Sailors' Stories   47

•

The

Sea

Has

Many

Voices

merely mocked him from airborne safety.

"So, think you're gonna eat me first, do you?"

Belly down on the steel plates, he studied the white mass beneath the buoy. The proprietary gulls settled down again on their perch high above him.

Shortly after midmorning, his gulls departed in a sudden flurry of wings. A few minutes later he saw why.

Another cruise ship, dazzling white with pennants flying in morning sunlight, plied rapidly on an easterly course that would bring her within a mile-and-a-half of his buoy. His sentinels took wing, lost identity amongst the melee wheeling and swooping—raucous squadrons quarreling over ship's offal. From the ship blared the sounds of spurious jazz.

The castaway shouted through cracked lips, waving, whistling feebly through unpracticed fingers.

"Helloooo there! Here I am; here I am! I thought you'd never come! Over here on this buoy!" He untied a cloth strip holding one of the clappers and with it began to beat the bell furiously.

He could see the ship clearly, her decks a soiled off-white, like the gull feathers. Passengers promenaded about in trim, light-colored clothes; some played shuffleboard, others lounged in deck chairs, while on the bridge paced a white uniformed officer. The ship's orchestra blared out a pseudo-jazz rendition of a Stephen Foster medley, replete with wailing saxophones and shrilling cornets.

"Help! Over here!" The castaway rang a frantic tocsin as the ship frothed abreast. "For Christ's sake, here! Here!"

Leaning on the ship's rail, a woman, who might have passed for black had she a slightly deeper tan, noticed him standing stark naked on the buoy.

"Here I am!" he shouted. "Hurry and tell your Captain." But the orchestra's din, the liner's thumping engines, and the swishing of the wake overwhelmed his shouts.

The deeply tanned woman pointed him out to acquaintances, who swarmed to the rail, gawking. Faces contorted into soundless grimaces of laughter; they nudged one another, gesticulating.

"Good God! You're not . . . you're not . . . abandoning me?"

The liner steamed on past. Gradually the rail people began to shrink, waving gaily; the deeply tanned woman fluttering a lace handkerchief. Gradually transforming into Lilliputians, the rail people became distracted by an argument on deck and turned toward it, no longer interested in the castaway's nakedness. With pennants flying the liner churned on eastward leaving the buoy dipping and pitching in her wake. While the castaway clung with both hands, the loose bell clapper tolled directly into his ear.

"Surely one of them—that officer, maybe,

must have seen me and radioed the Coast Guard. I heard that ship owners don't allow those big liners to be stopped or turned around for anything, because it costs too much. Sure, the Coast Guard'll be out here soon, all right." He searched for the cloth strip he'd used to restrain the clapper, but it had slipped quietly into the sea.

"Suppose nobody comes?" Receiving no answer he continued, "The Coast Guard maintains these buoys. What'd bring them out here to pick me up?" He lay back on the steel plates thinking, right hand stilling the bell tongue. In a few minutes he scrambled to his feet, climbed the ladder to the top of the skeleton tower, and beat upon the red glass lantern with the hilt of his sheath knife, chanting a recitative to accompany the blows.

"Someone"—smash—"will come"—smash—"when the"—smash—"light goes"—smash—"out," with extra emphasis on "out."

He climbed down, picked up the largest pieces of broken glass and tossed them over the side, then splashed away the remaining splinters with sea water.

When at last the sun slid behind the coastline, no light at all winked from the buoy into deepening gloom, and the white blob shimmered only dimly below the surface of the sea.

*   *   *

Darkness fell cool and rainy on the thirsty castaway, who managed a few palmfuls of rainwater. Soon the fog rolled in again, blanketing the buoy as it moved rhythmically in the slow swells. He slept, shivering.

Heading westward just before dawn, the same cruise ship inched through the fog on her landward journey. From even a few yards away her gala lights glowed but dimly and frostily. In her ballroom two dozen insomniac passengers still danced to musical platitudes of a bored and sleepy orchestra. Champagne flowed freely, and glasses clinked sharply amidst sporadic laughter. At regular intervals the cruise ship's foghorn emitted a deep groan that elicited no response, while in his cabin the sonar / radar operator swilled champagne and fornicated on the cabin deck with the deeply tanned woman.

Plowing through light swells at greatly reduced speed, the cruise ship neared the invisible red and black buoy and its sleeping occupant. From the ship's bridge a long shaft of light prodded the billowing white, restlessly wavering over the fog banks. All at once the ship shuddered, ground to a stop amid a cacophony of rending metal. A woman began screaming. The castaway awoke to the noise from the cruise ship, lights all ablaze. Suddenly the ship's lights blacked out, as if turned off by a single master switch. Voices shouted through darkness, carrying across the sea to the buoy and its aroused castaway.

Hearing such screams and curses, the castaway could merely surmise what was happening as the ship listed to starboard. From her slanting decks two flashlight beams glowed, playing fit-fully about breaks in the fog. The beams passed over one lifeboat crowded with people, another capsized with a dozen clinging to its gunwales, and another bearing one man and woman in evening clothes. All about the stricken vessel the sea teemed with thrashing arms, churning legs, bobbing heads. A fearful din of cries and screams filled the air. Now, above the cries a deep sound, as of a gigantic cello being crushed. At once the flashlight beams vanished. Through the darkness he heard a great bubbling, gurgling, and hissing followed by a moment of absolute silence.

A few moments later the castaway heard oars creaking in locks and indistinguishable human voices.

"Here! Over this way," the castaway called, striking the bell with his bludgeon-like clapper.

The rattle of oarlocks ceased abruptly. A long moment of silence followed; then, "Who's that?"

"It's me, over here on the bell buoy. You got a light?"

"No, my flashlight fell into the water. How the hell'd you manage to locate a buoy in this blackness?"

"I wasn't on your ship. I fell off a windjammer days ago and swam to this buoy." He struck a note with the clapper. "Home in on the bell. You're not far off." The bell clanged again. "Jesus, you don't know how good it is to hear a voice again—a real human voice." The dim silhouette of the lifeboat slowly materialized in the fogbound periphery of the buoy. "Here, toss me the painter!" He asked of the two faceless, obscure shapes, "Anyone happen to have a cigarette?"

A vague figure in the lifeboat responded, "I don't smoke, and Belle's still in shock. Anyway, she don't have her purse. Say, you'd better sit up front. That way it'll balance better. Careful now, can't see a thing!"

"Thanks," said the castaway, climbing carefully into the lifeboat's bow.

"It all happened so quick," murmured the woman. "One minute we're dancing, and then, all of a sudden...the ship stopped so quick it knocked me down! Whatever happened to Harry and Louise? Christ, my whole new wardrobe's gone..." her voice trailed off.

"It'll be daylight soon. How far you figure to the coast?"

"Maybe ten miles or so."

The woman said, "Wouldn't it be safer to wait here 'till daylight?"

"Believe me, lady, I've memorized the way to the shore. I been on this buoy for days and no one paid the slightest attention, even after I broke the red light."

"You broke the light?" the rower asked between oar strokes. "Ain't those red lights supposed to be warnings that something's under the water?"

"Yeah, sure, that's why I broke it—so someone'd pay attention!"

"Why, you selfish bastard; you sank us all just to save your own ass!" the husband stopped rowing. "All them people drowned!" In front of the big man the fog began to brighten. "And you even shut off the bell!"

"How many," asked the woman, "do you think got off safe? I saw hundreds in the water..."

"You gonna blame me for everything? Those big ships have sonar and radar to steer by, don't they? Why didn't...?"

"I don't know nothin' about that. All I know is you put out the light; you stopped the bell, and our ship sank!" The husband rowed more slowly, lost in thought. The woman buried her face in her hands. For minutes, for half-hours, no word was spoken. Little by little they neared the shore, while gradually the fog began to lift. The sky gradually became lighter and lighter. The woman, who had been drowsing, suddenly sat bolt upright.

She yelled into the half light, "A nigger!"

Her husband at the oars stopped rowing and turned around to look. "A bare-assed nigger!" He picked up an oar and aimed it at the curly head. "You sunk our ship, nigger!"

As a skilled boxer would, the black castaway sidestepped, and momentum carried the white man overboard. As the husband tried to climb back into the rocking boat, the black castaway

•

Gregory

Fitz Gerald

grabbed the oar and brandished it over the swimmer's head.

"No you don't! Stay right where you are and hang onto the stern. You make any trouble, and I'll bash your head in! I'll do the rowing."

The white man glared helplessly up from the sea, one hand gripping the stern.

"No use fighting it," said the castaway, beginning to row. "You can swamp the boat, but then we'll all drown."

The wife stared at the castaway, a strange look in her eyes.

"I can't help it," the black man said, "that I got no pants on. Nobody's making you look, either." At that she tittered, but boldly kept on staring.

When at last the boat bottom scraped the sandy beach, full morning had arrived, and only wispy patches of fog remained. As if at some prearranged signal, the woman began to scream at the top of her lungs. The white man stood chest deep in the shallower water and joined in.

"Help! Help! Police! This nigger sank our ship!"

The sea resort where they landed was deserted at this dawn hour. Above sea walls rows of peeling, warping cottages leaned woodenly against one another in morning sunshine burning through the thinning fog. The naked black castaway dropped the oars, jumped out of the boat, waded ashore, then ran up the beach and among the cottages as if on a touchdown run. The white man and woman kept on yelling. But by now the castaway had vanished into the still sleeping town. Church bells for early Sunday service began to ring. To this accompaniment curious, sleepy faces appeared at several cottage windows. All of those faces were black.

The title for this story is from T.S. Eliot's "The Dry Salvages," Section I, line 24.

Wreck of the Juniper

by Daniel Spurr

*A daring getaway by two young
lovers on a sloop in Maine triggers
a romantic mystery that lasts a
lifetime.*

IN THE YEARS before the war my father
owned a small sloop, which he kept on
a mooring in Seal Cove near the western
end of Eggemoggin Reach. Maine then was
not the place it is today, stained with trinket
shops and shoe outlets and gentlemen farm-
ers who have thinned our ranks like a rust
on the hollyhock leaves. But there were
signs of the southern invasion even in the
1930s and it brought out a mean streak in
my father, who by all other counts was a
peaceable man. To him Boston and New

York were foreign ports, and more than one yacht club skipper had his feathers ruffled when my father, furious at the helm of *Juniper*, maneuvered alongside their splendid yachts and hurled a volley of epithets that made a young girl like me blush.

So when I took up with a young man named Laddie, whose family vacationed on the cape, neither my mother nor I were surprised that my father forbade our meeting and, later, after I persisted, that he lost his reason altogether.

I was young and more than a little bored with the other boys in Brooksville. There were but three: Billy Thompson, with big ears and a sadistic penchant for torturing flies and frogs and just about anything else that hopped or crawled; Marshall Billings, a loud, fat boy given to pranks and bawling when his daddy whipped him; and Richard Lincoln, who might have been all right if he'd grown up anyplace normal, but there was little chance of that in Brooksville. One day he stole a pocketknife from Mr. Wainwright's store and was deported to a training school in Bangor. I didn't see him again for sixteen years, at my mother's funeral.

The first time I saw Laddie Angstrom I knew our futures were crossed. He was more mature than the other boys I knew, no doubt because he was a few years older and attended a prep school where they taught the classics. And he combed his hair back and tucked his shirttails in, which made him seem more polished than he probably deserved. Exactly what he saw in me I'm not sure, but then there weren't many girls in Brooksville either.

The particulars of our relationship are private and on occasion embarrassing, so I won't discuss them beyond saying that it was summertime, he was new, and I had never been kissed. By August my father had hauled me behind the woodshed more than once; mother cried and I swore I'd run away and make something of myself in the big city of Boston. The very mention of the word gave father a conniption and he would whack me again.

By August my meetings with Laddie were always clandestine, but with the damp woods and mossy rocks and moving water bearing on us like a wilderness, it wasn't difficult to meet in some secluded place where we were known only to the cedar waxwings and black squirrels and a bed of pachysandra. Then we'd hold each other and talk. Laddie hated the East Coast and longed for the brown foothills and dry skies of California which smelled of Asia, he said. The Pacific was a superior ocean, he argued, because of its volcanoes and cities and color, and even its name. "Think of Balboa," he said, squeezing my hand, "hacking his way through the jungles on the Isthmus of Panama just to *see* the Pacific . . . the Hawaiians who lie about all day and eat flowers and never grow old . . . the whalers' lookouts hanging on the yards shouting 'Ho!' when they spied a right whale's spout . . . and the Forty-Niners sifting for gold in the riverbeds. Imagine us riding the squealing San Francisco cable cars and strolling the Oakland docks where Jack London and the oyster pirates tore each other's ears off for bottles of rum! My god, Annie, the place is so alive the *ground* quakes with excitement!"

Truth was I'd never thought much about any-place other than where I lived, except Boston perhaps, and California sounded quite like a fairy tale—at least the way Laddie described it. Of course, he'd never been there either, but he said he loved the idea of it so much he was ready to hitchhike west at the drop of a hat. "What the heck, Annie," he'd say, pinching me, "let's do it!"

Perhaps it was because my father had such contempt for the other forty-seven states—with their presumed riches and decadence—that I began to crumble under Laddie's eloquent incitations. California was fast becoming the forbidden fruit. Laddie won me over completely when he said, "Besides, Annie, my parents have no use for me, and the school they send me to is dull as a morgue. And how 'bout you, huh? What sort of future do you have in these boondocks? Poetry will get you further than planting potatoes or chipping shellfish from some old dock piling."

We laid our plans by moonlight, on the top of a hill where we nestled in the crook of our special rock and he composed verses avowing our eternal love. I believed him, and though later my friends said I was a fool, they didn't convince me. At least not entirely.

It was on a Saturday morning, while my father and mother were doing their weekly shop in Ellsworth, that Laddie and I rendezvoused at Seal Cove for our getaway. He tried to kiss me among the wet pines but I was nervous and exhorted him to launch my father's rowboat post haste. We threw our satchels in and pushed off. Laddie, I was surprised to learn, didn't know the first thing about boats, and we were hardly off the shore before he had us spinning in circles. I had to put my hands on his to straighten us out and I think it wounded his pride a little.

Once aboard *Juniper* I took charge and Laddie seemed more than content to sit in the cockpit and watch me as I hanked the jib and bent the mainsail. About all I let him do was reeve the sheets through the fairleads but that, too, required explicit instruction. Finally I told him just to relax and leave the rest to me.

The day till then had been sunny and clear. In the southwest a few clouds were stacked like blocks over the Camden Hills, but I had little doubt we could reach Vinalhaven the first night. From there we'd run down Penobscot Bay to Tenant's Harbor, Popham Beach and on to Portsmouth, New Hampshire. Laddie said he had friends there who'd help us. When you look at the chart and the long witch's fingers of land scratching out from the mainland, there seemed little chance our parents could ever find us.

We cleared the heads at the mouth of Seal Cove and pointed high into a southwesterly breeze. Laddie started to joke about the shock of his parents when he didn't return for supper and for a time I was giddy with excitement. The meaning of what we were doing hadn't hit us yet, and on reflection I don't think it ever did. There was never the chance.

The fog came upon us quick as summer rain; one minute I could see the eagle's nest on Fiddle Head, the next nothing. It didn't roll in like it usually does, a convex bank of gray air with the delicately varied shadings of a storm sky. It simply materialized over us and all about the boat as if we'd sailed into the mist of a great waterfall.

That's when events started breaking down, self-destructing more quickly than we could put them back in place. Laddie grew anxious and took to pacing the decks for a glimpse of land. I tried to reassure him that I'd sailed these waters with my father for years, that if we were quiet we could hear the waves break on the rocks at Green Ledge, and if we simply watched the compass and measured the time on each heading, dead reckoning would eventually bring us to the bay. We'd recognize it by the bigger, longer waves, I told him, and there'd be a good chance of better visibility on the open water. I was grasping at straws, but at that moment Laddie was more of a problem than the navigation.

"Over there!" he'd yell, pointing at some illusory shape that was really nothing at all. Then he'd wheel about and yell, "No, there!" until I feared he was losing his mind.

"Laddie," I said as calmly as I could, "please sit and listen to me. The fog isn't necessarily *against* us. If we were rumrunners being chased by the revenuers, the fog would give us a welcome chance to escape, right? Our situation isn't so different. Now if you just pay attention to your watch we'll be out of this in no time."

We sailed on in silence. The benches were wet and our hair matted to our foreheads. When I reckoned we were free of the cape I altered course to the south, though the wind was light and I never was able to feel a change in the waves. Then the wind died altogether and I could feel the current pulling us back. The sails hung like skin from the bones of a corpse and the boom dripped like a gutterless eave. The fog lifted intermittently but not enough for us to see any land. The great circle in which we sailed would momentarily widen before contracting again so tight there was scarcely room to turn.

To say that Laddie had lost his enthusiasm is an understatement. The fog, it seemed, had found his Achilles' heel. He rubbed his hands and craned his head and kept saying, "I don't like this, Annie, not a bit."

"Sure, I'm scared, too," I said, though I never really felt it. To me the fog was the most natural thing in the world. Besides, my heart was too full of adventure and the life the future promised. My only fear was my father finding us and for that reason I found a sanctuary in that temple of pure whiteness.

When at last the wind filled in from the north, Laddie couldn't contain himself and went to the bow to look for treetops, which I said might be visible before rocks in the water. Islesboro should have been on our starboard beam, and it was, more or less. Without warning, the keel caromed off a rock somewhere north of Gull Point, catapulting Laddie over the bow. He had one hand on the forestay so that he swung over the water like a telltale behind the jib. For an instant his body was outlined on the backside of the sail. Then I heard him hit the water but couldn't see him. He never cried out.

I brought the boat up into irons and dropped the sails, which was the best I could do; there certainly wasn't any point in sailing to and fro among those rocks looking for him. I called to Laddie, oh, I called until my lungs ached. The only answer was the gurgling of wavelets against the beam. Then I collapsed in the cockpit and cried.

Eventually the boat worked its way into a crotch along the Islesboro shore. An overhang enabled me to climb off and for hours I worked my way among the rocks on all fours, searching and calling. At twilight I heard my name: "Annie! . . . Annie!" Then some lobstermen in a skiff appeared through the fog and I saw my father in the cockpit wearing a yellow slicker and a pair of binoculars slung around his neck.

Laddie's body was never found. Mr. Angstrom came to the house one day. Father disappeared into the woods out back, leaving me to
receive the poor man. Laddie had described him as
a self-righteous gent given to dry speeches about
capitalism and opportunity and using all your
brains and cunning to carve a ledge for yourself in
the mountain of life. This day, however, his head
drooped and his swinging chin seemed to cut an
arc on his sunken chest. "Just wanted to meet the
girl my son gave his life for," he said. He didn't say
much else really and I guessed he mostly needed to
fill in the last pieces.

The Angstroms returned to the cape two more
summers, then sold the place and we never heard
from them again. Later I heard a rumor that Laddie
had once stolen a car, and another that he'd gotten
a girl in trouble. Maybe they were thinking of me;
the folks around here tend to exaggerate, especially when it comes to scandal. Father managed to
salvage the boat. He hauled her on the Seal Cove
shore using a pair of skids and a pickup truck, and
after a few summers of work she was relaunched.
Despite his invitations I never again set foot on her
decks. She grew old with my father and one day
when the fog curled in off the Reach, he rowed out
to the mooring with a can of kerosene and a box of
matches. When the fog lifted she was gone.

During the war I worked at a shipyard in Bath
carrying rod for the welders, where I met Ruffy
Wilbur, who I married after V-J Day. We bought a
house outside Brooksville and my husband drove

his old Nash to the paper mill in Bucksport. Children would have sent my life in other directions, but a doctor told me I was barren as the rocks I walked on. Ruffy died in 1978 and I am rooted in this old house, stubborn as thistle.

Some days when the mood strikes I take out the letter I found in my mailbox a few years back, postmarked Los Angeles. No explanations. No justifications. No apologies. Just this poem.

*The color of blueberries you said varies with exposure
     to the sun and shale and their view of the bay.
What effect has the fog? I asked.
     None, you said, ignoring the sugar pop beading on
     your nose.
Light blue was all I ate sailing that ripe day when my
     ancestors shook pine cones from the conifers
And you made a wreath from them with cranberries
     and statice and the names that caught in your
     father's craw.
The water was cold, dear old Annie, and I got drunk
     as if I were swimming in highballs.
An olive caught me under the chin and superimposed
     your jaw against the varnished gunwale.
What effect has the fog? I asked. None, you said,
     though I knew it meant the difference between
     blueberry pie and Baked Alaska.
They serve jam and marmalade on this transcontinen-
     tal flight in plastic dishes that won't explode in a
     microwave,
And I see your face at 30,000 feet with cheeks puffed
     and a diary of rainsqualls in your eyes.*

So please send blueberries, toothworts and a piece of
Maine fog to press under waxpaper in my album.

He didn't give a return address, and even if
he had I doubt I'd have written. What would I have
said? As if he could make a difference in my life.

This cape was meant for me, the tidal flats
and gangly pines, the mica-flecked granite and the
delicious berries. During a spring low I can still see
part of *Juniper's* keel, jammed between two rocks
and crusted with mussels. But when I sense the fog
coming, and I can, I go the other way and climb the
gray escarpment behind the house. Below me the
feathered fog fills the draws among the hills and I
am never happier than when I descend into that
white-green quilt, feeling my way home by my old
feet and memory alone.

"Wreck of the Juniper" first appeared in Cruising World,
November 1989.

Flo

by Michael Badham

*During a severe storm in the
Charleston-Bermuda passage, a
skipper's aged mother-in-law
reveals another side.*

OTHERS-IN-LAW are traditionally the butt, and frequently
deserving, of mean-spirited
jokes. Mine was no exception.

Granted, Flo was an academician and
intellectual, and deserved respect for that.
But, on the other hand, she had all the
attendant flaws. In other words, she was
hopelessly impractical and quite the last
person one would want to ship with in a
vintage sailboat for the passage across the

"Triangle" from Charleston, South Carolina, to Bermuda—and in midwinter, at that.

Nevertheless, with the lure of a weekend's free hotel board and lodging for the children, Jean, and me when we arrived at our tropic destination, she suckered us into agreeing to take her with us. Diana, age six, and Jim, four, were delighted at the news. Grannie was putty in their hands, and they manipulated her shamelessly. She, in turn, hopelessly overindulged them, a practice I frequently and fruitlessly protested.

*   *   *

Our boat was *Westerly*, a 43-foot, half-century old ex-R.N.L.I. lifeboat used in the British coastal rescue service. She had been rendered ocean-proof for a recent trans-Atlantic passage from her home country to the Caribbean, thence to New England, and now south down the Intra-Coastal Waterway.

Flo, a recently widowed Australian, had joined us before we sailed from New York. She was committed for a few days, she told us, to researching Rhode Island's Roger Williams, so we were obliged to delay our estimated time of departure. Par for the course, I told myself; but we did have a little time in hand. Once we got under way, her principal chore was to take the washing to convenient Laundromats ashore. This she did in exemplary fashion until, one day, in a port-o-call named Dismal Swamp Canal, we became worried at how long she'd been away. I decided to go after her.

I found that when faced with two doors, one

marked "Colored," the other "White," she'd sorted the garments into two appropriate piles. In her outrage, on learning the true discriminatory meaning of the signs, she'd promptly marched into the "Colored" section breathing fire and brimstone, and had just as quickly been ejected. I soothed her ruffled feathers, and reminded her gently that, back home, she was a firm advocate of the White Australia policy, wasn't she?

Charleston, of course, with its stunning period architecture and gracious lifestyle, had Flo enthralled. Gentle citizens entertained us to a lavish family Christmas dinner, and Flo just couldn't get enough of the southern charm and accomplishment.

I delayed sailing, reluctantly, to allow her more time for her explorations. And then we were weather-bound for ten days on the run. The forecast was such that only an escaped criminal lunatic with the law breathing hotly down his neck, would have risked setting out for Bermuda at the time. Then, on Friday, January 12, we were promised a break for the following few days. Our crewman, Ed, a New York crane driver with no oceangoing experience but plenty of electro-mechanical expertise, had joined us by then, and we set about storing ship. Flo pleaded for yet another day in harbor to take the guided tour just once more, and I refused. Why couldn't she understand, I asked myself, that we'd been delayed long enough already, and were now seizing a chance to make a break for it?

•

**Michael
Badham**

I am not generally superstitious, but I cordially dislike beginning a sea passage on a Friday, a thirteenth or, worst of all, a Friday the Thirteenth. On this occasion, however, despite there being more bad weather forecast later, I calculated we could get across the Gulf Stream in time to escape it; but ONLY if we scampered away immediately, like on Saturday, even though it was a thirteenth.

After such a long delay, patience—and, therefore, good judgment—was wearing thin.

It was cold, damp and overcast, as we cast off from the Charleston Municipal Yacht Basin at 1000 the next day, bound for that tiny coral speck in the ocean, Bermuda.

* * *

I recalled setting out from England all those months ago.

"God go with you," a friend had called from dockside. "It's so much easier to be brave when the sun's shining, isn't it?" she added.

And so it had been.

How different it was, sailing from Charleston in bleak midwinter.

By 1630 on that first day, the wind increased to northeast, Force 5, heading us, and forcing us to steer 130°, well south of our destination. Pushing *Westerly* hard to get her out from under the lee shore hazard, caused her to pound mercilessly, doing no good to either herself or her crew. By 0200, the slowly veering wind was forcing us to steer *south* for heaven's sake! By mid-afternoon the next day, the wind had veered to south-by-east, had increased to gale force, and allowed us to thump ahead on the starboard tack on a course of 075°, roughly the right direction, at last.

With the weather as it was, I was at the wheel for most of the time, spelled for short periods by Jean and Ed. I asked Jean how her mother was making out. I was sure, by now, she'd be deathly sick and complaining constantly.

Jean raised her eyebrows, and shook her head slowly from side to side.

"Amazing," she said. "When she's not reading to the children, she's either helping Diana with her doll's washing, or teaching Jim how to tie knots. Not a sign of mal de mer. And," she added, "the sandwiches and hot coffee I passed to you awhile ago? She made them. And enough for the rest of us, without even being asked. She was even singing in the galley as she worked!"

"Miracles will never cease," I said, in wonderment.

For some time on the third day out, we'd been down to spitfire jib and reefed mizzen. During the night, under the glow of the red navigation light, the weather wrenched the port twin-staysail boom from its deck lashing. It cartwheeled into oblivion.

At 1330, or thereabouts, the weather deteriorated even more. The wind increased to Force 9. Visibility was nil as heavy rain beat down mercilessly. As I clawed down the mizzen, somebody yelled from below that the glass was dropping like lead.

The celestial pyrotechnics of the next four

hours were quite incredible. The rain was still torrential but, above to port, a smoky green sky burst constantly with blinding white and electric blue flashes. To starboard, the overhead was a bright, hard and glaring, yellow. Ahead it shone like burnished gunmetal.

It was as if the stage hands at a production of Gilbert and Sullivan's *The Sorcerer* had gone berserk with all the strobe lighting and gunpowder at their disposal. Sea height was (I'll swear) twenty to thirty feet, and the scene was lurid and fiendish to behold. The boat plunged and bucked like a crazed rodeo horse, and I shuddered to think what conditions must have been like below.

Hours later, the glass had steadied and there were a few clear patches visible through the clouds. The wind had backed to head us again, and it was pointless trying to make progress toward the east and suffer yet more agonizing pounding. So, I hove-to. With Ed at the wheel, I turned in to let the gale blow itself out.

* * *

Both the famed Welsh storyteller, Tristan Jones, and the experienced American passagemaker, Reese Palley, dismiss with ridicule the "Bermuda (or Devil's) Triangle" as a satanic manifestation of evil. They explain it for what it really is, an unfortunate melange of meteorological circumstances which sometimes combine to make life very uncomfortable for the mariner. Sailing on the thirteenth couldn't have helped matters and, of course, having a priest or strange woman on board was also traditionally bad joss. And Flo was strange, to the boat, that is.

As these thoughts were going through my mind, I was lying face-down in the head compartment wrestling with a recalcitrant rubber hose-end which refused to fit over its male metal counterpart. I heard a discreet cough behind me, and looked up to see Flo peering down, glasses perched on the end of her nose, eyes crinkled.

"Er, you know, Mike," she said, "if you were to submerge that rubber end in boiling water for a short while, it should then be malleable enough for you to fit it in place."

And it worked, just like she said it would. I was grateful, and said so, though a tiny bit resentful that it was my head-in-the-clouds mother-in-law who had to show me the solution.

By now, I'd had a restful sleep, and we were reaching along happily under genoa, main, and mizzen in a Force 4 out of the northwest. I'd been able to shoot the sun and, by noon, calculated we were 500 miles from our destination, which we were fetching on a course of 097° true.

But the respite was not to last.

It wasn't long before Ed and I were doing hourly tricks on the manual bilge pump. We were taking on water and we had an engine oil leak. A tide of oily bilge water sloshed over the cabin sole. Flo, to my amazement, was magnificent. Not a word of complaint as she waded ankle-deep through the sluicing mess, cheerfully helping Jean keep the rest of us supplied with food and drink. Laughingly, she conceded that although this wasn't exactly "yachting" as she'd pictured it, things were quite a bit better than the "Mayflower conditions" we'd endured earlier. The children pitched in and helped wherever they could. No complaints from them; but then there never were.

On the eighth day we picked up Gibb's Head on Bermuda's southwest corner. We had no engine power, no electrics, and a fresh offshore breeze. *Westerly*, however, was not renowned for her windward ability.

It was peaceful enough, though, and that evening we gathered round the deckhouse for a glass of wine.

I looked at Flo, and asked, "Is there something about you we don't know, but should? I mean, the way you've handled all this has been, well . . . "

She smiled, said, "Cheers," and sipped her wine. She then drew a deep breath.

"All right," she said, slowly, "I've never talked to anyone about this—it's too painful. I've tried for many years to put it out of my mind, more or less successfully, I think. Perhaps the time has come. You see, well, Diana knows this—I was married for a short time before I married her father. What she doesn't know is how my first husband died. She's always been told it was because of a car accident. Right, Jean?"

Jean nodded, her expression growing more baffled by the minute.

"George and I were fanatics about sailing," Flo continued. "In fact, we spent every spare minute we had during the six short months of our marriage cruising the New South Wales coast in his Folkboat, a small lapstrake wooden sloop with an auxiliary. We got to know that boat and all her foibles, inside and out, even in such a short space of time. We loved her."

Flo turned to gaze toward the flat outline of land to our north. With her head still averted, she continued in a small voice, "Anyway, what's been so hard to live with is the knowledge that it was all my fault . . . all *my* fault." After a pause, she turned back, and there were tears in her eyes. "It was I who made him do it; it was all my stupid, ignorant impetuousness."

After a pause Jean put an arm round her; she cradled Flo's head into her neck.

"Go on, Mommy," she said, "if you want to, that is." Then she gestured to the children, who were silent, looking at their grannie curiously.

"But what about . . . ?" she started.

"They're growing up to be sailors," said Flo, shaking her head. "They know already that sailing's not all sweetness and light. Let this be part of their extended nautical education, a cautionary tale, if you like."

I refilled the glasses; I had to do something

with my hands. Then Flo, more composed, began quietly.

"We'd had supper at anchor in Jervis Bay, you see, about a hundred miles south of Sydney. It was a gorgeous night, and I thought it would be lovely to have a moonlight sail up the coast. But George wasn't so sure. The forecast for the next day was for a norther. George asked, 'What if it's ahead of schedule?' But I cajoled and pleaded, and said how romantic it would be. Then I got a bottle of champers and some *foie* from the icebox and, well, after a while, he agreed. I could be very persuasive in those days," she added, smiling softly.

"So," she went on, after a pause, "we set off, and the storm did arrive ahead of time—and it was a screamer. By 0400, we were hove-to under a wisp of canvas, the forestay parted, and the mast came crashing down. It carried away the guardrail to which George's safety harness was hanked, hit his head a cruel blow, and sent him over the side into the boiling sea. I screamed after him, appalled, as his lifeless body drifted away to disappear in seconds."

She was silent again, head turned, reliving that hideous experience.

"Anyway," she went on, looking up again, "I just crumpled up on the cockpit floor for I don't know how long, weeping brokenheartedly. Within an hour or two, I think, the storm passed, and I knew I had to pull myself together. I set about clearing up the shambles, had a cup of tea, then started nursing our little boat up the coast under power."

She was dry-eyed as she finished her story, and even managed the hint of a smile as she said, "Now, perhaps you can see why I'm reasonably at home in small boats. Also," she added, more quietly, "why I've never felt able to tell that story before, even to Diana."

I put my arms around her, and gave her a long hug.

*   *   *

By early morning, Ed had worked his magic on the engines, and we slowly closed the entrance to St. George's Harbour on the island's northeast corner. As we rounded the Spit buoy, I called down to the saloon for Flo.

When she came on deck, I showed her where we were on the chart, and our destination.

"Care to take her into harbor?" I asked.

She smiled and nodded as I gestured for her to take the wheel.

I went forward and busied myself with the holding gear.

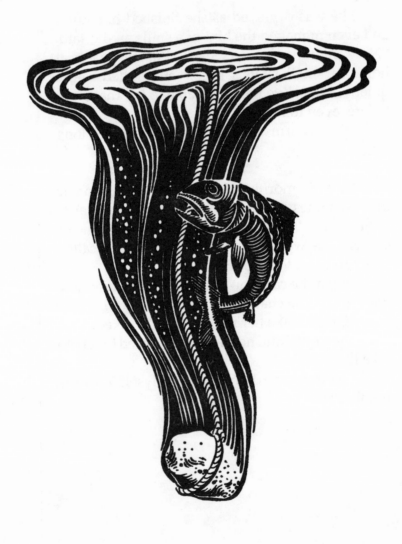

Foggy Foggy Dont's

by Mary Lee Coe

*Despite misgivings, a mother puts
her faith in her daughter's seamanship as they set out to find their
anchored sailboat.*

DARCY, UP TO HER KNEES in
water, holds the dinghy steady as I
climb in. I don't ask her the question that pounds at me as I crouch my way
to the midship thwart: How will we ever
find Nat in this fog? Though he's less than
a mile from here, he's behind a wall of
white, and night's falling fast.

At least we know he'll stay anchored.
It's one of the rules about sailing in fog he
was telling Darcy just this afternoon as we

drew closer here to Quahog Bay. "Foggy foggy don'ts," he calls them.

"Why do you call them that, Dad?" Darcy asked.

"You know," and he sang a chorus: "Just to keep her from the foggy foggy dew." Then he said, "Oh yeah," at Darcy's blank stare, realizing that at seventeen, her musical knowledge hardly included the Beatles, much less Scottish ballads.

Then, "Don't go anywhere, stay put, first rule in fog," Nat said, scanning the attenuated belt of white far away on the eastern horizon shrouding Junk 'o Pork Island. It meant fog tonight, but it had rolled in far sooner than we'd expected.

And now Darcy and I are breaking Nat's first "Don't." But we can't stay here on this island; we rowed over when it was clear, in hardly more than our bathing suits. The fog took us unawares, shrouding our shoulders while we were crouched over the mussel-bed gathering dinner.

Now it's like a damp quilt, smelling of wet concrete, and I shiver as Darcy wades away from the dinghy, stooping now and then to search the bottom with her hands. Suddenly she stops, feeling something, then pulls a potato-sized rock from the water. She crooks her arm at me and I pole the dinghy toward her. She wades to the bow and says "You row." Then tying the end of the bow line around the rock, she starts measuring the line by holding the rock straight out with one hand and pinning the rope to her chest with the other. She knots it, then divides the remaining line into three-foot segments the same way. After she marks them all with knots, there look to be four or five yards.

She's so intent; I don't ask her what she's up to. But it's not easy feigning faith in her seamanship. This pasty air is totally disorienting. It's futile to yell—although sounds carry, you can't figure their direction. Nat's second *Don't* is don't trust sounds. Still, I want to shout, scream, do something, just to hear Nat's voice.

"Okay," Darcy cocks her head over the water like a heron. I look and don't see anything. Here and there a slight breath riffles the surface, but the damp air has deadened the wind. The shore has disappeared. We're alone now in a tiny circle of black water.

I try to comfort myself with the thought that Darcy's seamanship is second-nature: I was five months pregnant with her when we sailed through a hurricane to bring Nat's boss's boat back to Maine from Bermuda. Darcy must have taken to all that pitching and screaming, the crash of thirty-foot waves over the deck, the feel of me fighting for balance. Ever since she was born, she's loved being on the water.

But seeing her now, I don't know. She's fingering the bow line, puzzled. Her face, pale around the eyes where her sunglasses have been, is frozen in concentration—the way my stomach feels.

Tiller and the Pen

At last, she climbs into the dinghy. Water sluices off her calves onto the coiled bow line as she kneels in the bow thwart.

"Okay," she calls, "pull on your right oar. That's it, now straight, okay, now pull together just like that." She navigates us through the thick cloud curling like exhaust over our gunwales.

"Stop," she says after a few minutes. As we drift, I turn and see the bow line paying out; Darcy's hand guides it below the surface of the water. Then she looks off into the fog. "See that?" she points.

I shake my head. I can't see anything, except that it's getting darker.

"Off to port; see the ripples?"

I put on my glasses and stare hard at the water until I see them—slight ridges of gray on the black surface. "Yes."

She follows them with her eyes to our stern as we drift. "Now, row parallel to them; keep the breeze on the port beam."

I turn my back to her and pull hard on the oars, keeping my head down. I don't want to see it growing darker.

Darcy reads my mind and says "Don't worry. Dark doesn't matter in the fog."

My silence isn't fooling her; she's taking care of us, and we both know it. I row harder; at least I can do this, give muscle to her navigation. I'm not good out here; I can't balance, and I hate windshifts. But I can make my arms pistons that won't quit, my chest a vase of steam. I dig the water furiously, plying the oars like pitchforks, till my palms stick to the handles.

Darcy finally says "Okay," and I turn, breathing hard. She's paying out rope again.

She has me feather the surface slowly, while she dips and pulls at the stone under water. I picture people on the street outside Portland Institute for the Blind tapping their white canes along the curb. Finally I say "What are we doing?" trying to keep desperation out of my voice.

"There's a sandbar running halfway across this bay," she says. "I saw it on the chart. It'll be about six to eight feet under us at this tide. Dad anchored our boat just inside the southeast end of it. We'll row 'til we find the bar, then turn left. And follow it."

"But what if we row in circles?" I say.

"The wind's about southeast, I think. If we keep these ripples on the port beam, we'll bump right into it."

I don't ask, but she sees me raise a finger, feeling for the wind.

"It usually won't change direction in fog," Darcy says. "And we're lucky; it's often dead calm in this stuff," she lifts her hands at the gauzy air. "But see?" She points to a zephyr brushing the water.

I'm glad *she* can see it.

She keeps her hand on the line, feeling for the sandbar. I remember Nat marveling years ago, when she first started taking the helm. "She's a natural," he said, referring to the optimum angle of wind and sail she always found. "It's in her hands."

I hope her magic holds for a bar underwater, because my own senses, as if shut down by the loss of one—my sight—can't resolve this scene. Each impression remains separate, isolated. There's no summation. The white all around makes the dinghy seem motionless; I have to bend and see bubbles flying from the oars to believe we're moving. And the muffled grunt of our oarlocks, the lisp of water against our bow, resound as if in a white wind tunnel, seaming us in. Is the dinghy, the water, the misty figure at my back, are they real? Am I going mad? "Darcy!"

But she doesn't turn, and I suddenly see her back rigid, her knuckles white on the gunwales. Boils on the surface of the water scatter the regular ridges of wind.

"Tide!" Darcy cries, pulling up the line and motioning me to row hard. "I can't see where the wind is anymore, Mom, so stay on course. Keep her steady as Steely Dan—we won't see the wind again till we get across this tide."

I bend over the oars and make the dinghy fly for what seems the length of a football field. Darcy finally calls to me to slow, and begins to take soundings again. As suddenly as it had deepened, the water shoals—ten feet, six, then "Good!" Darcy cries, as my oars catch sand. "I know where we are now. Pull on your left oar."

I do, churning sand up against our gunwales.

It reminds me of Nat's last foggy don't: Don't set a course to a gradual shore, because you might run aground. My futile strokes roil up more sand, then suddenly we spin around and are off the bar, back into deep water.

"Okay, right only, yes, that's it," Darcy says, then "Good, keep her straight." Next, I hear her call a long, triumphant "Eeeee *yew!*"

I raise my oars and turn, don't see anything, then hear a blast of horn off our port bow. Darcy raises her fist, motioning us forward.

"Yea babies!" Nat yells, and suddenly all sensation comes together. I feel the muscles moving smoothly on my bones to take back the oars; I see the fog growing thinner, more luminous. I cleave the water with perfect flex, and in a few more strokes Darcy says "Here!" and we come to rest against our yacht's hull.

Nat leans down for our line. Darcy unhitches the rock, tosses the rope up to him. "Think I'm gonna keep this," she turns to me with the rock. I squeeze her hand then look past her, to Nat.... The fog opens for a moment, showing a patch of early stars behind his head. Darcy backs up from the bow, letting me pass.

I take Nat's hand. It's warm, a perfect fit. As he hoists me aboard, I feel like I'm climbing into the sky. The hibachi glows on the stern rail, Darcy climbs aboard, and we're home.

A Daughter of the Tradewind

by Richard Morris Dey

A young lady captures the fascination of all who cross her path until she herself comes face-to-face with "Paradise."

"Another country heard from."
—Clifford Geertz

S HE'D COME OUT HERE "to try out her luck"—was that it? I heard the rattle of a tamarind pod pass by and looked away from the hotel, harborwards through the palm fronds, out into the hard, unremitting glare. Boats of all kinds tugged at their anchor lines and nodded to the tradewind that came in catspaws gusting across the dazzling, blue-bay waters.

I'd been trying to find her and when I heard she wasn't around, I found myself asking, "But has she left the islands for good?"

"Who the devil cares?" an old acquaintance had challenged, downing a Guinness Stout. "What are you, her brother? Forget that one. You've been north too long, Red. There are plenty like her about. Too bad you didn't take her on the *Henrietta*, eh?" He picked up his empty boat bag and started toward the open market. "Say what you like. Her only problem," he finished, "was to find another boat."

In the veteran view she was just one of the scores who drift in and out of a place like this, seeds on the wind. You see them all the time, the makeshift travelers making-do, their backpacks the only baggage of their wandering. Mayhew would say the backpacks brim with dissatisfaction, vague ideals, unspoken sorrows.

"What do you suppose that one is looking for?" he'd ask. Melissa was like them and not—I knew that much right away. Her course had run in counterpoint to mine in our early days out here— not that I, a fair-skinned, flatfooted redhead ever threatened to steal the limelight.

When I first saw Melissa I stood right where I am now, all eyes and ears and hopes, as if in coming out here like a seed myself I had escaped the hothouse of mainland living, gone beyond the boundaries of prescribed cultivation to grow.

"I know just what you mean, Red," she'd said after we introduced ourselves. "Anything's better than . . . but let's not talk about that—not *here!*"

She'd arrived on the mailboat that afternoon with a flute and a friend, and was only too glad to see the "boyfriend" go his own way.

"Imagine," she said in an accent of the Commonwealth, softly, "imagine not being a free-spirit in a place like this, at my age!"

She raised the flute to her moistened lips and started to play.

"New talent!" one bandanaed bystander muttered slyly, his eyes drinking her in, widening. And though she claimed not to know the first thing about boats ("I've always been a city person, Red"), I saw the other yachtsmen notice her right away too.

She looked the part to live the island life, all right, and carried the silver flute like a talisman in those early days. And when she played that flute the island was hers for the asking; seemed reflected in the bays of her clear blue eyes. It was green then, and tasted of mango and lime, and smelled of frangipani and other blooms whose names I hadn't yet learned.

Melissa found work easily in the charter business, first as a cook ("Isn't everyone a graduate of the Cordon Bleu?"), then as a deckhand. Quickly she proved herself a natural on boats, one with all the right responses and grace. And what she didn't know, she learned fast as I well recall having taught her myself the half a dozen knots a sailor needs to know, how to change a fuel injector ("Wait, I'll get it, Red. *There*—it's not so hard, really!"). Once, we studied celestial together and marveled at the clarity of this southern sky as we worked out our sights, and at the Pleiades in particular as if we could navigate by their brilliance alone.

Soon Melissa was hired as skipper of a yacht owned by an industrialist from the States. Or was it Greece? It hardly matters for he seldom used the schooner. ("It's quite like having my own boat, Red, my bloody own. And to think I once had a 'proper' job!") Few would deny how masterful she was with *Halcyon*, sailing these island seas, never striking a reef or blowing out a sail. The troubles normal to a complicated wooden boat in a place like this never seemed to cramp her style.

"A lucky lady," one had murmured.

"A lady who knows her business," someone else in that expatriate cluster had said, looking at another who only glared as if with too much rum or not enough.

"Clearly," Mayhew said, "the owner's got money . . . but wait," he added mysteriously.

In the tourist season she did day charters for the hotel guests who said they'd never forget the sailing in these waters—nor Melissa, I thought. She was the very image of that person every guest would like to be if they could stay and not return to their mainland worlds.

"You, you're doing it!" the businessmen would say. "And having the time of your life!" But something in their tone, as we caught it, was less than sincere: This was just a playground to them and from the bar, adjacent to the dining tables, we'd overhear their wives say, "What in God's name *are* these people doing? They don't seem to have gone 'native,' Dear. But thank God we didn't raise our children to fall into this . . . this frivolous existence!"

At that time I was mate aboard a private yacht and no matter what anyone said, Melissa was beautiful to see running that schooner. When, in the late afternoon light, she tacked under full sail into the wide bay, you could just make her out braced at the wheel, holding the wheel a spoke down, with the decks slanted and the lee rail awash, the two of them, schooner and skipper, hard to windward. She'd tack a dozen times in her taut approach, each time closing the distance, growing larger. People stopped along the foreshore to watch, mesmerized by the driving image in partial silhouette driving over the calm, iridescent waters. And after tacking precisely to a spot only she could see, she'd shoot the schooner up into the eye of the wind like an arrow and let go the anchor. The headsails slid down their stays. She'd back the large mainsail then, and let out chain until they came to rest with the whole fabric of the tall schooner quivering.

"Red!" she'd sing out, putting up the awning, "Red, whatever *are* we doing out here!"

The parties were unrivaled aboard *Halcyon*. I can remember how artful she was with everything in its proper place (except, of course, for the glasses

Tiller and the Pen

and bottles and the way some of us ended up overboard, swimming naked), and how elegant she was on deck and below in the soft flickering glow of kerosene lanterns, all of her kept meticulously as if the schooner were indeed Melissa's, her pride. In this harbor forested with masts, many without apparent distinction or purpose, *Halcyon* under Melissa was like a clearing in the woods.

Work as she did to maintain the white schooner, Melissa still found time to practice her flute. And she spoke often enough to believe it of wanting someday to compose music for the BBC ("I've had tons of formal training, you know.") It seemed this living—braced, as it were, at the wheel with all of her self-possession and spontaneity—this life lived at the level of art was, while living for its own sake, yet a kind of digression for the sake of something else ("And won't we be the richer for it, Red!"), however long the digression might go on.

In this shimmering plenitude of light she'd flourished to become the consummate island sailor. And you could see her depart the island with the same skill ("Dat one got plenty nerve, mon!") she'd brought the *Halcyon* in with: With the anchor just breaking free, she'd fall off the wind, filling the sails and weave downwind playfully amongst the anchored yachts. This was something of a show but everyone did it or wished they did, and gybing a heavy gaff-headed schooner in winds like these is no easy trick even with a handy crew. ("Another thing I've learned, Red, is a boat's got a soul—a soul—quite as surely as you and I!") And so, with the morning sun striking the sails set wing-and-wing, they, growing smaller, more distant, would run south or head up and beat north off Frenchman's Table. It seemed the land had no claim on them, none, as surely as I'm sitting here now.

There were sometimes reports of the schooner being in three different places at the same time—St. Thomas, St. Lucia, and Aruba, say. But the sound of Melissa's flute gusting downwind over the blue bay seemed present wherever (and with whomever) I happened to be, reassuring and far reaching as the tradewind itself. Once, when Mayhew asked about her and us, I allowed we shared a certain kinship. That much was true. But after a time we'd kept a distance between us. "We're too alike," she had parried gently, making light of making love, "to be anything more than we are, Red. It's already too much like incest!" If I thought anything then, I suppose it was simply that like all of us out here she was keeping her options open. And why not?

It was in March or February when Melissa, taking on water in Kingstown, received the telegram:

SCHOONER SOLD STOP
NEW OWNERS ARRIVE
IMMEDIATELY STOP

In Trinidad at the time, I first heard the news from a Bequia man and had worried about her.

"It mus' be she go bottom," he'd told me.

"What?" I'd asked.

"Sink, mon—she gone!"

Melissa, it turned out, was paid off hand-somely and promised another boat said to be cross-ing from the Med. Again the island welcomed her and she welcomed it, saying the job had gotten "too formal" and that she'd grown bored with boats anyway.

For some time then she lived along the water's edge, a kind of soldier-crab hanging out at the harborside hotels. I saw her more often in those months playing backgammon and chess through the lazy afternoons, paling around into the night with the other yachties and some of the more cosmopolitan locals. Day or night everyone con-gregates at this hotel which is situated like a stage to the surrounding amphitheater of hills. Every-one caught up in the chance events of their impro-vised living exclaims how "dreamlike" or "like a movie" the scene out here is. No one wants to leave, everyone contrives to stay— "Traffic? Starwars? Monday?" they ask. "Think Barclay's will notice an expired Visa card?"

Mayhew (with his sympathetic yet faintly sardonic smile) would say that despite the palmy ambiance, it's not unlike a merry-go-round here: always the same scene revolving to the usual mu-sic, seductive and numbing, with the faces seeming in their blurred, hypnotic turning never to change.

"And isn't that the point of it?" he'd ask, pulling at the wide brim of his salt-stained straw hat, "that in a place like this you can be any one you want with any past or none?"

But I could not have remarked this myself, then; nor did I have the faintest clue to the secret of Mayhew's own survival running his *Island Seas*. This was still a place something like Paradise, and not to me alone.

For on those magical nights that *were* like the movies, Melissa, playing "Marianne," danced as if the film would never end, shaping the space we all lived in, and I can see her to this day tanned and sultry, dancing in the fierce glare of Tilley lanterns and wearing tortoise shell bangles. On those evenings a bloom of bougainvillea would be tucked in the round braid of her curly hair blowing in the gentle winds that held her unconcealing blue cotton dress before them like a spinnaker. And wasn't she just one of many then—then and now? I guess!

As it happened there was a piano here and sometimes, between sets when the steel band was resting, I would accompany her. My hands were stiff and rusty as old iron gate valves and it was all I could do to keep up with her, with the silver flute when she got "hot, *hot*, mon, like de sun!"

She had a natural ear and could pick up any tune and run so far with it that when she resumed her dancing you weren't aware the flute had stopped. The guests recorded her, estate owners asked her to dinner, yachtsmen to their yachts, and everyone would offer to buy her drinks, meals, anything. Even on the beach she wanted for nothing, I'd think wryly, counting my BeeWee dollars.

Day or night, it's true, her eyes did glance seaward as if she were expecting someone, a ship to arrive. But that is the common gaze out here, and I thought nothing of it. There was always something in the offing for all of us, and no one doubted that when she was ready to move on she'd flute her way into the Andes, across to Papeete, on to Bali or Kathmandu. And, in time, to London or L.A.

It seemed right as the wind that she'd go on like this, impervious to the glare, running before the wind, on the everlasting edge of it, for as long as she willed or wanted. It seems right now.

* * *

"You're not still lookin' for that one, are you Red?" Sydney asked, passing back through the hotel. "You'd think you were still starvin' on yachts, Red!" His boat bag brimmed heavily with pawpaw, cabbage, and eddo. "There's a jump-up tonight at the Sugarmill, and Desmond says he wouldn't mind you stoppin' by later. Have you seen the piano he's got? Nothin' like that old wreck you used to beat on here. Maybe she'll turn up again, like she used to, eh? What was that tune you used to bang out together?" he pressed. "How did it go? 'If you leave me now, you'll take away the better part of me...' Somethin' like that, wasn't it?" He shifted the weight of the bag to his other hand.

When I didn't respond, lost as I was in the palm shadow overlaying the harborfront, in the blue-white glare, he demanded "You *do* still hammer at the keyboard, Red, don't you?"

Those had been inspired times with Melissa gusting on her silver flute and the crowd dancing, having a fine time around our impromptu interplay. But I remember how in odd moments I'd hear a flat, bad note while working those ivory, warped keys as if to warn that almost anything sounds good in a place like this, that you'd have to record the atmosphere itself to get what you think you're hearing.

"But seriously, Red, a drink? How's L.A.? Even out here we get your tapes."

The clouds that scudded overhead strangely intensified the glare and made it thick and grainy, without shadow or light. "Sure," I replied at length, and we went to the bar where I recalled another sound, how sometimes in place of her flute on a still mid-afternoon I'd hear a telephone ringing across the harboring bay waters, mysterious and disquieting because it went unanswered. But no one I knew of was trying to reach me then.

"Even out here, Red, we get your tapes," Sydney repeated. "Charterers bring them. I don't suppose you'd be where you are now if you'd stayed in these waters, with boats, eh?"

"Probably not," I said.

Later I returned to one of the Adirondack chairs and watched Sydney untie his dinghy from the hotel dock and proceed (in his dark glasses and faded surfer's T-shirt) to slow-speed out toward his shimmering white ketch.

Had I never seen Melissa again, I might well have gone through the Canal myself, west to do whatever in the way of running boats would earn a dollar. But I did see her. We met on the public road winding up from the waterfront. It was the dry season then, and in the glare I saw Melissa was not the same.

Not a fortnight earlier I'd gone to look her up at the house she rented with her soldier-crab friends. I was on the beach myself then, desperately low on funds and wondering what to do, to travel west (I'd met a well-known yachting author, been asked to sail with his family to New Caledonia), to stay put (to work for Mayhew, maybe), or return to what I could hardly imagine, so complete had my own adaptation to the light out here been. Harsh as it could be, the sharp bright dazzle of it and the blazing deep colors of the things that grew under it seemed right to me in a way the more muted and often artificial, colder light had never seemed back ... home. This was something Melissa, unlike the others, understood. I could always talk with Melissa.

Smokin' Joe was there and two French-speaking Chinese, a Pakistani, several from the Commonwealth, and others from the usual Western capitals. But no one seemed to know where Melissa was. "Yah," one said, "she liff here, sometime."

And the one called Smokin' Joe: "You need a place to crash, mon?"

The house was set back one hundred yards from the beach, behind a barrier of seagrape and mangrove trees. Behind it a hill rose sharply and the light filtered down through a tangle of branches and vines. Off the path to the house was a well, partly boarded over like a hatch-top. It was a single story, modern place. Inside geckos leapt at flies landed in the deflated folds of backpacks, and the air smelled sweetly of burning mosquito coils. The bodies of those present shuffled by like cows grazing.

Outside, posted on a machineel tree, was a sign: "This house condemned. Idlers keep out."

"There's room here, mon, plenty room," Smokin' Joe said.

"Right, right," I replied in the lilting island intonation.

In a rumshop one day I was playing dominoes in the West Indian way—*Slap! Slam! Slam! Slap!*— and losing more than I was winning. I had wondered aloud where Melissa had gone.

"Yo' does be lookin' lost yo'self, Red-mon," the proprietor offered above the voice of the government radio station proclaiming in an interview with a visiting Rotarian "de tree S's—de Sun, de Sand an' de Sea!" He was a large, heavy man with bloodshot, friendly eyes who also ran one of the island's funeral societies. He explained, "Yo' pays but one dollah on de eve o' de full moon, an' we takes good care o' yo'. Miss Melissa," he added, "she already join!" *Slam! Slap!*

After working for a week on a banana estate, I heard the beach house had been raided by the local gendarmes to root out any illegal aliens, and that Smokin' Joe alone had been spared the indignity of jail. "They weren't looking for Melissa, Red, or you, were they?" Mayhew had wanted to know, pulling at the wide brim of his old straw hat. "And about Melissa, when she had that schooner: Was she meeting up with someone for purposes having nothing to do with chartering? Could she have been trapped, doing not what she wanted but what someone else wanted her to do?" His eyes were all bunched-up at their corners and tired. "Did she have too much of a good thing, maybe play too many for too long against one another, trying to stay unassociated? Where did she go? Do you know, Red?"

We'd been standing on the deck of *Island Seas* and when we went below I said, "You know as much about her activities as I do—more, probably."

I was beginning to see that whatever she did, my interest was more in what she wasn't doing and in why.

Mayhew asked, "Was she too beautiful, Red? Was that it?"

* * *

"Well," she said on the public road when we had met and stood facing one another. "See what the wind's blown in. You've heard the BBC is coming out here, have you, to make a film on island sailing, how it's everybody's dream? Maybe," she said, blowing at a fallen strand of her curly blond hair, "we can do the music together."

Melissa stood in the glare in a patched flour sack dress. She was thinner than she'd been aboard *Halcyon,* and I thought the rumor about her having had an abortion induced by an obeah lady might be true. Her arms were black and blue and rashed, reminding me that Mayhew had said her "boy-friend" had returned briefly. A few flies circled about one of her ankles bandaged, in gauze. And her eyes, sleepless from the ankle's infection—her eyes in this sailor's paradise were brown with living reefs.

"Actually, I had hoped," she said, attempting a straight smile, "you wouldn't catch up with me." Like the soldier-crab without its shell, her whole countenance begged for anonymity. "But a funny thing, Red, is that I've never felt 'invisible' the way you say you sometimes do out here."

I started to ask her something but you could say our kinship spoke for itself. And yet she seemed to know something I did not, something she didn't want me to know, perhaps. She pointed vaguely with a chunk of silver fish toward a ridge to the northeast and said she was lying low for a while and mumbled something about a need to sort things out. I saw the lips she had tried to moisten were cracked. Watching my eyes watch her, she added: "For Christ's sake, Red. We know the light out here is smashing but by itself," she softened, "quite overwhelming, really."

"And the flute?" I asked.

"I sold it."

The heat that day was staggering. It seemed the wind had passed the island by.

Starting up the hillside, she paused and turned. "Life's not art, Red. Make no mistake. It may be like art, it may even be better than art, but it's not art."

That heat, rising from the hot, glary macadam Melissa then limped away on, rose languid and wavy about her, floating her like an island on this island sea. But in the hand that had held the flute, I saw a tamarind pod jerk, heard its dry seeds rattle, heard again her whisper: "You want me, I know, and I still want you, Red. What a time we could be having. Christ!" she'd said. "But one of us someday has got to get back and it won't be me, Red. You have something I don't, some kind of faith— or will if you can survive this place and this light and me."

At some point I'd heard she was in need of a skipper—or, more accurately, a mechanic foolish enough to imagine that by his tinkering he could keep afloat a sinking basket case if ever there was one, one hundred twenty feet of neglect waiting for the mercy of a chainsaw. I swear you could see right through her planking honey-combed by worms, straight to the harbor bottom. Her three masts were checked deeply, her sails unstitched or stolen, her slack miles of rigging hardly fit for tuning. She didn't even have a wheel—just the bronze wheel shaft turning, unturning with the windshifts shifting her blurred, blistered hull. She'd been around for as long as I could remember, most of the time careened and worked on as much by the elements as her local crew. No one— "You might as well swim away from here as sail on that hooker," Mayhew had said—wanted the job, a delivery north.

Derelict as she was, she seemed some time later just the thing for me and I went right to work on her. No sooner had I done one project than two more appeared, and I really wasn't sure I'd ever get her away. She beat the beach-house, though.

Looking for Melissa, I'd gone back a second time and seen no clock then, only a scrap of singed paper dense with crabbed arithmetic. There were empty bottles and vials and no chairs, reggae and rock tapes but nothing to play them in. Barely a map of the island hung on the cracked, turquoise walls. What breeze there was nudged pages from an unglued paperback. I saw moths dead at candle stubs, their dismembered wings carried off by ants. It was like seeing a river bed in a territory you thought you'd never set foot in, a broad dry flowing without banks or source that seemed in whichever direction you looked to merge with the horizon.

I kept half the harbor up most nights running *Henrietta's* pumps, and was forced finally to set sail when the island ran out of the petrol that fed those

wheezing pumps. Why the owner wanted her, I
didn't ask. His agent had said: "Get her to
Martinique, first. There's a railway big enough for
her in Fort de France, I hear."

Once Melissa had turned off the public road,
I never saw her again. But even then I'd gotten the
hang of freedom. That, I suppose, was my luck.
Had she been too beautiful for having faith in her
gift—faith and the discipline it takes?

"I have it," she told me sometime after the
glare had burned through those harboring,
unharbored eyes. "I know how art's sense is itself
an experience, like making love or sailing well. But
I don't trust it or maybe I can't live up to it . . . .
Christ, Red. It's not me."

And clear to me as it is that our counterpoint
stopped when I took command of the *Henrietta*, it's
impossible now not to hear on this tradewind
sounding through the green fronds fronting the
glare, the sound of her playing the silver flute—or
someone like her. For along the water's edge it's
said Melissa left eventually for St. Kitts (or possibly
St. Barts).

"There's a big regatta up around the Saints,
remember Red? A different sense of space."

---

*"A Daughter of the Tradewind" first appeared as a narra-
tive poem in the author's collection,* The Bequia Poems, *
published by Macmillan Caribbean in 1988.*

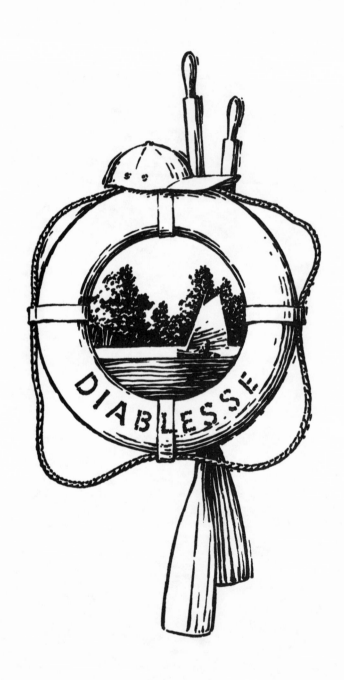

Cruise of the Diablesse

by Tamsen Merrill

*Daydreaming of earlier times and
larger waters during a sail on a
pond changes a woman's direction.*

ESTHER WORTHINGTON now made
a weekly ritual of the excursion in
the sailing dinghy. She had become a
familiar sight to the boys at second-string
soccer practice. The team captain called
Mrs. Worthington "a tough old bird," add-
ing, "sexless" under his breath. While the
players scuttled up and down the field, she
marched along the bridge to the floating
dock, an oar in each hand. She wore
a duck-billed straw hat. Her gray hair

protruded from its edges like frayed manilla rope.

Esther did not often dwell on her emotions. But, as she prepared for her sail, she mulled over the morning's events. Something had interfered with her progress to the millpond and she could not put her finger on what it had been. At the market she had stopped for rice, toilet paper and winter bird seed. On the placard for the renovated building next door she had noted with concern that a Dr. Coddle, psychiatrist, had opened an office. To Esther this new presence betrayed a weakness in the fabric of the town. Just as a consulting Ph.D. was not necessary to determine that a tomato plant had root fungus, a psychiatrist was not required to detect a human problem. If it was real, the problem would manifest itself and something could then be done about it. In fact, psychiatrists sometimes created problems, just to stay in business.

From the market, she had walked to the post office to mail those books to her daughter. Phil, the postmaster, had raised his eyebrows when he read the address on the package she pushed across the counter.

"Yup. Betsy's in Alaska now," Esther had stated. "She's researching Arctic moles. She got herself a grant from one of those science foundations."

"Hey, isn't that something!" said Phil.

As she left the post office, Esther had bumped into the young wife of the new history teacher.

"Hello, Esther," the woman had said, "What's new?"

Esther remembered she had struggled for an answer, but not what she had replied. She wished she had left the house earlier to avoid confrontations with people whose names she could not recall.

Now Esther stepped solidly into the middle of the dinghy. Yes, that's what had interfered; that cheery, "What's new?" It was only in the last five years as she revived some habits that Esther had begun to feel truly centered again. In contrast to her daughter, who was perpetually trying new things, the centering had turned Esther toward the past. Why should there be anything new? For punctuation she dropped the oars into the bottom of the dingy with a clatter.

The migrating geese that stopped in an un-used corner of the athletic field with their outlandish honking, had a routine similar to Esther's. When the lingering fog clouded her path to the compost pile in the spring, she immediately began plans for her trip to the lake north of the border. There, with her old friend, Becca, she canoed about and caught landlocked salmon. Later in the year, when the snow fell on the pond and made skating impossible, she hopped a plane to Florida to visit her ailing brother, arriving unannounced in her slicker and Wellington boots. Otherwise, she never crossed the town line and preferred the garden in summer and the wood stove in winter, to human company. This included, she had come to realize, her husband. His death had entailed an adjustment of her habits, sometimes difficult. But now, after five years, she concluded that his absence was convenient.

As the academy physician, George had devoted himself to the school. He set broken legs, gave flu shots, coaxed quiet boys out of their shells and coached the cross-country ski team. He was most loved by the students for his ability to reassure parents about the fitness of their sons, despite evidence to the contrary. Even Esther could see the pervasive effects of drugs in the boys' "dead-fish expressions" and in the way they giggled when there was nothing particularly funny. But, to George they were just fun-loving kids and wasn't it great how things had not changed since his own school days at the academy when they had water fights in the dorms.

Esther kept George's house clean and cooked satisfying dinners. In his most affectionate moments he would comment on her sturdiness and how much it impressed him. More often than not he attended meetings at school in the evenings. In the fall he took freshmen on a three-week wilderness camping experience. During the early years of their marriage, George often proclaimed it a stroke of luck that Lou Davenport, class of '39, had introduced him to Esther, a woman as self-sufficient as his own mother had been. In the later years, he had told her that he never wanted a life different from the one he had with her.

She had settled for the silent dinners, the evenings spent reading by the fire, the shared chore of shoveling snow. Father had pointed out the obvious fact that she was no beauty and had counseled her to choose a husband with her heart, and most of all practically. No one else had presented himself, so George had been the most practical choice. She moved with him to the town where he had grown up. Like most of her classmates, she had never considered pursuing a career outside their home.

Having fetched the sailbag and life preserver from the boathouse, Esther rigged the dinghy exactly as the instructor had taught her on the beach on the Island, many years before. In those days all the children who summered along the beach sat in a circle as he drew with a stick in the sand to illustrate tacking, sailing before the wind, broad reach or close hauled—a language that Esther had absorbed like the sun.

A musty odor now wafted from the water of the town millpond. Its border stretched from a pine shore to the soggy edge of the academy playing fields. The stream at one end and the dam by the foundation of the old mill made a poor circulation system, Esther thought, compared to the healing wash of ocean tides. At this time of year, a leaf landing on the pond at the stream might take an hour to make the passage in the current to where it would catch on the edge of the three-foot high dam, until a wave slopped it over the concrete onto the rounded stones below. Today the breeze would be enough to carry Esther contentedly tacking from shore to shore. The sky streaked with mare's tails seemed to forecast the pretty arc that would soon be in her sail.

If she maintained this dinghy, it would not have mildew spots under the seat and the sail would not be missing a batten. She considered offering her services to the school. The dinghy was used only occasionally, on weekends, when the older boys invited local girls for a sail because the gunwale concealed them from the waist down. Esther had watched one negligent couple from the dock on Saturday. The wind caught the forgotten sail and pitched it across the boat. Two heads disappeared, replaced by two pairs of kicking feet. That wanton display did not irk her. Esther didn't care about such things. The trouble was that the couple disregarded the most rudimentary elements of sailing.

Her schedule did not include time for daydreaming. For Esther, a brisk sail on a fall day was a healthy engagement and no one could fault her about indulging in idle pastimes. But, today the sun was a trifle warmer, the odors of fall a little more ripened, so that Esther became less clear-headed than usual.

How had she done it? For thirty years of marriage she had eliminated all thought of sailing until just this year, when on impulse she had borrowed the school dinghy. Of course, there had been those involuntary urges to stir each spring at the end of Betsy's school year, at a time when Mother would have whisked the family off to board the Island steamer. But such instincts, like those of the migrating birds, were simply seasonal.

As for George, the closest he had ever come to seamanship was in the collecting and polishing of brass objects. After his death, when the church bazaar volunteers rang her bell for white elephant items, Esther found herself pressing a brass ashtray, never used, into their eager hands. Once begun, she continued, giving objects to the school, to the children of neighbors, to the postman. She once sent a lamp to a man she had met on the plane to Florida whose address she had got because he said he liked Brussels sprouts. Now all the brass was gone. Sometimes the house seemed pleasantly airy, like a beach cottage on a summer day.

She remembered as a child how her heavy wooden boat resembled a sea turtle drawn up on the shore. Finally freed from their lesson, the children dashed to raise the colorful gaff-rigged sails which began to snap in the wind, carrying the boom careening back and forth. With a push off from the beach and a turn of the rudder, the sail filled. Esther's boat cut proudly through the choppy harbor. A reflection of flawless red paint outlined the hull's passage.

She won almost all the races. In the winter a

blue pennant for each victory decorated the wall of her boarding school bedroom. Now the pennants lay pressed beneath a girl scout bugle in a box somewhere in the attic. Maybe I should hang them in the living room, Esther thought, as the water spun from beneath her rudder.

The dying wind carried the sound of a whistle. Esther glanced up to the soccer field where the play had stopped momentarily. The boys in their striped uniforms looked silly as they started again, chasing back and forth the length of the field, land-bound like the shore birds which scurried on the beach at the whim of the waves.

On the tiny pond Esther's sail went slack. Her memory took her to other times and larger waters, to races when the strands of her salt-soaked hair stuck to her cheek and she leaned way back to keep her little boat from tipping too far and shipping water. Right off her leeward side was her nearest competitor, a chubby blond boy. She delicately eased her bow off the wind to correct a shiver in her sail and to steal more of his wind. Squinting against the spray, she focused on a marker ahead and ignored the droplets of water that entered the collar of her jacket. She felt it happen, but did not watch, as the boy slipped into her wake. With precision, she rounded the mark and headed downwind at a gallop.

In a sheltered corner of the beach house porch, Mother waved a victory signal from over her afternoon tea. The small cannon on the race committee launch announced Esther's passage over the finish line while the white caps on the harbor slapped her hull in congratulations.

Each year when she returned and launched her freshly painted boat she found the harbor sands had shifted. The tide had cut new channels. Beaches had developed fingers or their edges had been sculpted back into graceful curves. She studied the harbor floor, peering through the shallow water to discover hidden passageways that would give her the advantage. In a race, at mid-tide, she knew a rival would run soundly aground, while she—passing only a minute later might slither over the same shoal with a thumb's-width clearance beneath her rounded hull. She could almost feel the tickle of eel grass through her planks.

But now, adrift with the fall leaves, Esther had lost her bearings. As the pond grew more placid, her thoughts returned to rougher waters, long forgotten.

She was at the helm of another boat, the *Diablesse*, on that final cruise, the one before the move inland for George's appointment at the academy. Fred Holcolm, just out of medical school, was a new acquaintance for Esther. He had invited them along for the weekend on his family's ketch.

"Keep her pointing. You'll find she'll balance. Does he always get this sick?" Fred asked with a nod toward the cabin door.

From below they could hear George vomiting up his lunch.

"I don't know," Esther replied. "We've never sailed together."

Ahead in the darkening afternoon was the harbor entrance. A marker light winked from atop the west jetty. For the last hour it had been just the two of them on deck, attending to the creaking boat in a heavy wind that threatened to become a howl. As they turned at the final buoy, she watched Fred's strong back as he trimmed the sails, until *Diablesse* was over on her ear, causing a stream of water to rush along the leeward rail. Now he sat just forward of her, with his back breaking the spray that would have soaked her. She gripped the tiller in both hands, her feet braced on the opposite seat. By playing with the straining rudder, she found the boat's balance and eased the hull through the harbor entrance just as if *Diablesse* was a new born babe slipping from between her mother's legs. Sailing was the most glorious thing that one could do and the *Diablesse* was the champion of boats.

The shore began to block the wind.

"Guess it's time to get the anchor ready," Fred had said, with reluctance.

Then he had turned to look for a moment, right into her eyes. It was the same admiring look he had given the *Diablesse* that morning when they had approached in the rowboat. Esther's cheeks turned red. She raised her hand in an attempt to arrange her hair, blown into tangles by the 25-knot wind.

"You did a fine job getting this old boat in

here," he said into that terrifying silence.

George's head emerged from the cabin. His face was yellow.

"Where the hell are we?"

But Esther, full of strange emotions, could not answer her fiancé.

Then the dinghy hit the dam. The mast snapped and pierced the water. Although unhurt, Esther was covered by the sail as it billowed down. She struggled from beneath as if from under bed covers. Pond water filled her canvas shoes. The old sail gave a hearty rip as she clambered over the boom and onto the cement wall. From there she turned to survey the extent of the disaster.

Slimy water rushed into a jagged hole in the side of the dinghy. A smell of decay entered her nostrils and made her feet unsteady, just for a moment. The dinghy slumped lower, plywood groaning against cement. As the water rose, covering the seat, Esther understood that her mistake had been much greater than allowing herself to daydream on a fall day. It had been years in making, but its revelation made her shiver. She suddenly recalled the shock of when she had seen Mother and Cousin John kissing in the pantry. How happy and humming Mother had seemed afterward whereas before she had seemed one of the gloomier people of the world. Yes, thought Esther, and all this time *I* have missed sailing on the ocean.

"You okay?" came a sudden voice.

Esther turned and saw a line of boys in shorts

and knee socks balance along the dam. The one who had spoken to her looked a little like George. She was about to apologize for her negligence when she realized that the boy was really not much older than the chubby blond one she had beaten so often in races long ago.

"Foolish pond wind died on me," Esther explained. "The centerboard's stuck and the boat's missing an oarlock, so I couldn't row."

The entire second string defense was required to pull the submerged dinghy from the pond. With long sticks the offense retrieved the oars and life preserver which spun in circles near the dam. Through all this, Esther remained silent. If she had been alone, she would have left the dinghy to sink into the murky pond, but out of politeness she waited. When the job was done, she thanked each player and shook their hand. Then with her back straight, she left. Some boys snickered at the sucking noise her shoes made as they pumped through the mud.

Esther did not care. She felt a fresh southwest wind at her back, carrying her along. In her head she was listing things to do. Call the steamer dock for the schedule. Find Mother's old binoculars, somewhere in the attic. Were they in that canvas bag with the conch shells? It wasn't the season and the summer houses would be all boarded up, but that didn't matter. She was off! Off and sailing to the Island!

Island Hunter

by Christine Kling

A waitress in search of distant
horizons invests in a relationship
of promise.

*I*MOVED IN WITH JACK three days
after I met him. He sat at a table in my
station and began drawing on his napkin. Just three days later I hung up my two
uniforms in the boat's hanging locker,
stocked his ice box with my Kern's guava
nectar, and picked up my own key to the
showers from the boat yard's front office.
At the time, I was determined not to fall in
love with him.

Not only was I glad to be out of the
Inn, because living and working at the same

place starts to feel dirty after awhile, like inbreeding, but I felt like I'd made it inside, finally. I'd been drifting up and down the coast, working at the places in the marinas mostly, trying to slip my way into the boating world. Boat people pretend it isn't true, but really, as far as they're concerned you might as well be invisible if you don't have a boat or live on one.

When I was a teenager, I used to read all those true story accounts of people who had sailed around the world. And I daydreamed. I imagined every detail of my islands and what it would be like, sailing in and dropping the anchor through the darting colored fishes to the bottom of my own blue lagoon. Jack may not have been the man of my dreams, but I hoped he would get me there.

I shouldn't even have been working that day because I had switched over to nights about three months before. But when Darlene asked me to cover for her, I said "sure." I didn't mind the sunrise shift, especially on those winter mornings when the air was so clear you could see the Channel Islands rising out of the Pacific like a sharply focused picture. Every hill and gully was so clear you could almost count the goats on Santa Cruz.

I noticed him right off when he walked in. Grungy jeans and paint-spattered Topsiders. Only the cane he used made him atypical of our clientele.

"Are you ready to order?" I asked him, pulling the pen out of my ponytail.

"Yeah," he glanced at my name tag. "Tova, I'll have the special, over-easy."

I usually hated to have customers order the special because it meant they'd be straight ten-percenters. But it was slow and I was curious about the drawings on his napkin. My dad used to leave the same sort of doodles on the pad next to the telephone, especially after long, late-night conversations.

"Is that a cutter rig?" I pointed to the napkin.

He really looked at me then, not as a waitress, but as a person. His eyes, pale green, like the color of the ocean when the fog's really got you socked in, weren't even checking me out like most guys would. I didn't know what he was looking for.

"Yeah, you're right," he said. "Do you sail?"

I shrugged. "I used to. Oh, you know, just afternoons with my dad. Down in Newport Beach, we'd rent a Lido 14."

"Did you like it?"

"Sure. My dad would tack his way through all the moored boats, past the Balboa Ferry, out to the jetty where he could see the open ocean. Then we'd talk about where we'd go someday when he would sell his store and buy a cruising boat."

"Did you ever go?"

I shook my head. "He died first. He would've though. If he'd had the time."

He nodded. "I've just about got my boat ready to go cruising." Then he smiled and I could tell from the wrinkles at the corners of his eyes that he was quite a bit older than me. Late thirties, I guessed. "As soon as the boat's ready, I'm headed south. Then I'll follow the easterly trades. Mexico, Polynesia, New Zealand. Then I'll either come back because I'm broke or continue around."

I knew I had to get back to work and I'm usually pretty good at coming up with witty part-ing-shots, but I couldn't remember any of my lines. He'd just spoken my dream out loud.

In the kitchen I was standing, waiting in front of the toaster when Lil came in and nudged me with her elbow.

"I saw you in there talking to table number three."

"Never hurts, right?"

She broke the stems off several bunches of parsley. "He's a regular. Been coming in here for years. Watch out or he'll be bending your ear all morning with that sailboat crap."

"I can handle it." I knew it could take a long time to get a boat ready for the open sea, and it seemed I had met Jack at just the right time. Be-sides, I figured Lil's idea of a great guy was one who invited her out to Pro Wrestling.

Dad would've liked Jack. I mean he looked nautical, like a younger version of those little carved wooden sea captains they have in all the marina gift shops. But his beard wasn't white. Remember when you'd drink milk as a kid and you'd get a milk moustache? Jack's beard and moustache were almost all dark brown, but right around his mouth there was this fringe of golden hairs. He looked like a big bear with a honey moustache.

And of course there was the cane. He'd hooked the crook of it on the window sill before he slid down into the chair, keeping his right leg stretched out straight. He was sitting there, sipping his coffee, and sometimes he'd look up from his drawings and stare out the window at the islands while his fingers were tapping out some simple rhythm on the wooden shaft.

So, when I came out into the dining room later and saw he had finished and left, leaving his drawings on the table, I grabbed at the excuse to chase him out into the parking lot.

"Excuse me," I called out. He was already halfway down the drive to Pacific Coast Highway. "You forgot your drawings."

He looked up at me as I jogged down the drive holding the drawings in the air as though they were some kind of winning ticket. He smiled. I knew he'd meant to leave the drawings and he knew I knew.

"Thank you," he said. He folded the napkin and slid it into the back pocket of his jeans.

"Well," I shoved my hands into the pockets of my apron, jingling the coins from the morning's tips. "Good luck on your cruise." I started walking back up the drive.

"Hey Tova," he called. "Down at the boatyard in the marina, I'm on the *Island Hunter*. Come by sometime. Ask for Jack."

He waved and I started to wave back, but he had already turned around. He wasn't limping at all. He used the cane more like a walking stick, barely leaning on it, as he turned south toward the marina.

I couldn't have stayed away from that boatyard. I couldn't stop thinking about him the rest of my shift. I couldn't not go. Here was a real live person, not some character out of a book, who was going out there, going to sea, sailing to my islands. And if we didn't get along, if things didn't work out, there would be other boats. At least I would be on the inside.

I rode my bike down there that same afternoon, after I'd showered and changed. The Anacapa Inn is up on this hill overlooking the pier north of the marina, and out to sea I could see a white blanket of fog was being drawn in to the coast, ready to tuck the town of Ventura in for the night.

I was able to coast almost all the way to the entrance where the sign said, "Channel Islands Boatworks. No Unauthorized Personnel Allowed Beyond This Point."

Here there was something more than the usual salt-tang seaweed smell that you breathed throughout this town. Here was dust from grinders, diesel exhaust, paint spray fumes. Just beyond the sign there was this rotten-looking skiff up on an old trailer with two flat tires. About six guys were either sitting in it or leaning up against it, drinking beer, talking, and smoking. I didn't even realize Jack was one of them when I walked past trying to look "authorized."

"Tova?" He stepped away from the group. They all stopped talking and watched us as we said our hellos. Then one of them murmured something and they all threw back their heads with explosive laughter.

"Hey Jack," this big guy with long dark hair waved his Coors can at us, "don't go making any promises you can't keep." His dark lips curled back in a smirk.

"Later you guys," Jack said. As we walked away their talk started again. "Don't mind him." Jack led me into the shadow of a big power cruiser. "That's just Indian Bob. He hasn't exactly got both oars in the water."

The guy didn't look like a lunatic, but I figured that maybe Jack was one of those guys who couldn't take a little ribbing about his success rate with women. It did make me uncomfortable though; I always felt lonely when groups of men laughed in that intimate, locker room way.

"Come on," he said, "she's over here." He walked over to this big wooden boat and pointed up at her with his cane.

"*ISLAND HUNTER*," he said. I was startled to see her up out of the water like that, her dried, brick-red bottom nestled into the wood cradle.

Somehow, I had expected to see her in the boatyard's slip, straining at her docklines, ready to go. He showed me the long spruce mast resting on sawhorses beneath the boat. I didn't want to walk under her; in spite of those heavy wooden arms, she looked so tentatively balanced on that narrow keel.

Jack was talking about how she had been built in Norway in the thirties, thirty-eight feet of double planked oak, a strong boat.

He hooked his cane over the inside of his elbow and he seemed to have no trouble bending his knee as we climbed up the tall aluminum ladder. I wondered then if it was some kind of trick knee that could suddenly go out on him, or if maybe he thought women went for a man with a cane, like some women are turned on by eye patches or shaved heads.

In the cockpit we were at eye level with the second story of the marina office. Jack wiped his feet on a scrap of lime green carpet that covered the teak cockpit floor. Then he led me down below and I fell in love.

I didn't know much about boats really, except what I'd read in the books, but when I stepped into that warm wood cabin, saw the tidy bunks, touched the polished brass, I knew, I knew. I was going.

"I hope to get out of here by February. I think I can finish the mast and get her rigged in four months."

I stepped into the galley, strapped myself in

and tried to imagine cooking on that tiny stove at a thirty-degree heel. "You going to singlehand her?"

"Sure, if I don't find crew." He was sitting at the chart table running his fingers over a chart of the Mexican coast. I unhooked the galley strap and leaned over his shoulder. He turned his head and suddenly our faces were very close. "But, I wouldn't mind taking along an extra hand," he said.

White tufts of fog threaded their way through the masts and rigging out in the harbor. We sat in the cockpit. Jack made some joke about needing to warm ourselves up when he brought out the bottle of tequila.

When we climbed into his bunk a few hours later, I was less drunk than I had expected to be. I wanted to touch him, hold him. But we talked a long time before we touched, exchanging hopes and histories. After we made love, Jack slid down and rested his head between my breasts and sighed. I lifted his hair with my fingers and rubbed the top of his head with my chin. I touched the golden aura around his mouth. The sex had been good—we had each found our moments of pleasure. As my heart slowed, however, I found myself dreaming of a landfall on a lush island where brown men walked barefoot and sliced open cool drinking coconuts with machetes, where they sang songs at night in odd minor harmonies and drummed the earth with their bare hands.

My schedule at work was perfect for Jack. We got up, and over coffee and toast, we discussed the projects we would be working on that day. I sanded and varnished and cleaned up after Jack until three o'clock. All the aft floorboards had been removed so he could work on the rebuilt engine he was installing. We stepped around tools and balanced on the beams that supported the floor.

It was tough getting dressed in my white uniform, pulling on panty hose and tying the bow to my apron in the boatyard's dirty, unisex shower stall. My hands were dried and cracked, my fingernails cut to the quick; but it didn't really matter to me. I was going somewhere, finally. When I would get back to the boat after my shift, at midnight or one in the morning, Jack would always wake up when I climbed aboard and, wrapped up in my grandmother's quilt, looking like a patchwork monk, he'd kiss me hello. Then we'd empty my tip money out onto the table and count it out, discussing whether we could afford the good alternator or whether we should order the new storm sails.

"But there's a set of storm sails on the boat right now, isn't there?" I'd ask.

"They're over six years old."

"Well, how many times have you had to put them up in six years?"

"Tova," he opened the quilt and pulled me in next to his warm naked body. "We're putting our lives on the line, here. It won't take us that much longer to save up the money."

How could I argue with that?

Jack had money. Not much, but he did get a

monthly disability check. I had to ask finally, about the on-again, off-again limp. He told me he used to work construction. He'd been working down in a ditch and the guy on the backhoe didn't see him. The bucket had crushed his knee before the driver heard his screams and backed off. He had a couple of steel pins in there, but it had healed well and he said it almost never bothered him. He'd grinned when he said it was about the best thing that ever happened to him. "I bought the *ISLAND HUNTER* with the settlement check," he said. "Nowadays, I just keep the cane to keep the checks coming in."

"So it's basically a scam?"

He looked straight at me with those cool green eyes. "Sometimes a person's just got to do what he's got to do to make a dream come true."

I understood what he meant.

That group of fishermen and boatyard cronies always watched me cross the yard to the shower when it was time for me to go to work. One afternoon, as I was waiting my turn outside the head, Indian Bob came up beside me and crushed a cigarette under his heel. "Where are you and Jack going, once you launch the boat?"

"South, Mexico. But I'd like to see the Channel Islands first. Jack says they're so beautiful."

He snorted a laugh. "He should know, right?"

I was beginning to understand what Jack meant about this guy. He rocked from one foot to the other as he spoke, looking everywhere but directly at me.

"I don't know what you're trying to say."

"Six years Jack's owned that boat." He turned and spit a tobacco wad in the dust.

"So?" The door to the shower opened, and a young man hurried past us leaving the way open for me to go on inside. But for some reason, I wanted to know what Indian Bob was getting at. "So what?"

He rubbed his hand across his mouth and I could hear the raspy sound of his beard stubble against the rough skin of his palms. "Don't know what he's been telling you honey, but far as I know, he ain't left the harbor yet." He barked out a laugh, hiked up his pants, and returned to the group around the skiff.

I hurried into the shower shed, locking the door behind me. I pulled down my jeans and tore off my shirt. I made the water as hot as I could stand it and scrubbed my skin red.

I heard Jack's voice in my head, telling me about Smuggler's Cove and the cave close to Lady's Anchorage. Jack had talked about all those places as though he had been there. But then I told myself, Indian Bob's half crazy, Jack said so. There would be other boats now that I was on the inside, but somehow that thought didn't make me feel any better.

The day we test-fired the engine, she lit off at the first turn of the key and Jack let out a whoop and did a little soft shoe with his cane up in the cockpit. He'd stuck a garden hose up the engine water intake. As I waited to see if it would flow out the exhaust all right, I shouted up to Jack that it looked like we were giving the boat an enema. I heard Indian Bob's laugh from across the yard, but Jack leaned over the side of the boat and looked down, tight-lipped. Something in his eyes scared me a little.

But the engine ran beautifully and we did celebrate by quitting early and walking out onto the jetty with a bottle of Andre champagne. I felt great, both because of the engine, and because I had the night off. We jumped from boulder to boulder, dodging the spray that sometimes flew into the air when a large breaker crashed onto the rocks, and laughing when the salt mist stung our eyes. We snuggled together in the lee of a particularly large boulder and popped the cork.

Jack hoisted the bottle. We hadn't bothered bringing glasses. "To *ISLAND HUNTER*. And Tova. Two fine ladies." He reached into the breast pocket of his flannel shirt and dropped something small and cold into my palm: a tiny gold dolphin.

I bit my lip as he removed the light chain I always wore and threaded the dolphin onto its length.

"How does it look?" I asked, fingering it where it hung in the hollow at the base of my neck.

He kissed me. "Just right."

"Thanks Jack." We sat for a while then, just listening to the splash and pull of the waves on the rocks.

"So Captain," I tugged playfully at his beard. "When do we launch?"

"End of November, maybe." He handed me the bottle.

"Come on, let's set a date." I drank fast, trying not to taste the stuff.

"No way." He grabbed the bottle from me, startling me. "You set dates and they always come and go in the boatyard. Besides, I've been thinking that as long as she's up there, I might as well drop the rudder and see if I can't improve those bearings."

"What? Jack, you can always improve things on a boat. If we wait 'til it's perfect, we'll never go."

He lifted his arm off my shoulder and climbed to the top of the boulder. His back was to me when he said, "So you're the expert now," and the wind whisked his words off making his voice sound muffled like a bad connection.

The sun was setting behind Santa Cruz Island and the sky was a maudlin pink, like a scene on a tourist shop trinket. I walked up behind him and slipped my arms around his waist. My heart was thudding, echoing inside. I pressed my face between his shoulder blades and breathed deep of his salt and sawdust smell; it seemed to fill that place inside that had suddenly seemed so hollow.

I pointed out to sea, at the islands. "We'll stop at these islands first, won't we? I look at them every day from the windows at work. We've got to stop there first."

"Sure."

"Tell me about them. What's it like out there?"

"It's quiet. And clean. There are only a few people on Santa Cruz, ranchers mostly. Nobody lives on Anacapa. The shoreline is raggedy and rocky. Lots of sea life. Seals, whales, otters. If you can stand the cold water, you can dive for abalone."

"You're kidding." I slid around him and kissed him gently on the mouth. "I love abalone."

He smiled. "No, I'm not kidding." He looked over my head and the sky gave his skin a rosy glow. "We'll do that. There's nothing like fresh ab. The pinks are best, but they're mostly gone now." He lifted my hands from his back and led me back down to our champagne bottle. The granite felt colder when we sat again.

"Mmmm. Fresh abalone. God, they don't even print the price of it on the menu at the Inn anymore. When we have it, it's about thirty-two bucks." I took a long swig from the bottle.

"Yeah. Thank the environmentalist assholes for that. Save the otter and destroy the abalone."

"Oh Jack, come on, that's bull and you know it. I'm just as responsible as the poor otter, the way I gladly shovel the stuff out at the Inn because I know people who eat abalone are usually good tippers."

"Just don't go calling them 'poor otters' around Carter or Indian Bob or any of the other ab divers who hang around the boatyard. Those guys carry rifles on board and they shoot any 'poor otters' they see when they're out diving."

I knew I was drunk then because I started crying. It was just so easy for me to picture it, a little otter swimming on his back, his dainty paws pulling the white meat from the pearly shell, the crack of the shot, and then red, red, spreading in the water.

"Jack, they're ruining our islands. They're ruining them, Jack, before we ever get there." I tried to see his face, hoping to see the truth there.

"We'll get there," he said to the wind.

Waitresses make good tips on the holidays. Especially at the Anacapa Inn. Tourists and locals would come to see the Christmas decorations on the lawns above the Pacific. I had asked Darlene to schedule me for six nights a week, and what with working all day in the boatyard, I was really beat. The only way I managed to keep going was because I had this place inside me that I could crawl into when it got really bad. My islands. The hostess would seat me five tables in a row, the line at the bar would be six waitresses deep, the cashier at the front desk would make me wait while she talked to her boyfriend on the phone, and on and on. Wait, waitress, waiting. And I would go visit the barefoot men, drink coconut milk, and swim with them in the clear warm water.

On my break, I'd take a cup of coffee and go upstairs to the linen storage room that was directly over the entrance to the Inn. There was a small window I could slide open for fresh air, and I'd lean back against the stacks of folded napkins and breathe in the fresh sea air mingled with the dry, linty smell of linens. I liked to watch the different people coming to the door, especially those that used the valet parking. I watched them smoothing their clothes, adjusting their furs, as they climbed out of their plush automobiles, laughing, the women mostly wearing gold, sometimes jewels. They looked so free, like they had no place they had to be, only where they wanted to be. They were coming to the Anacapa Inn especially for the abalone and they didn't care if the price wasn't printed on the menu.

We launched the boat on Christmas Eve. It was supposed to be quite a celebration. I had the night off and we had even made reservations at the Inn for dinner. I'd be working on Christmas day, so, we figured this would be our holiday meal, and if we ordered the special, we could afford it.

They shackled these big straps under the boat and lifted her free of the cradle, then they just drove her over to the water. It looked so weird to see the *ISLAND HUNTER* flying through the air like that. Jack jumped aboard as soon as she was floating to see if she were taking any water. He poked his head out the hatch a few minutes later with a triumphant grin and signaled the crane driver with a thumbs up.

I climbed over the lifelines and went below to the ice box. I'd got up early that morning while they were preparing to launch the boat, and I'd raided the geranium beds at the marina entrance.

"Congratulations, Jack." I draped the slightly bedraggled lei over his head and hugged him.

"Thanks," he said. "But we'd better check out that pump. There is some water in the bilge."

"But you expected that, right?"

"Yeah, I expected that."

It was Jack's idea to try out the engine that afternoon, to take the boat for a little cruise around the inside of the harbor and run the engine up to full RPM for a bit. What I knew about engines wouldn't half fill a Dixie cup, so I mostly just tried to keep out of the way and jump when he said jump.

The yard guys threw off our lines and Jack backed the boat slowly out of the slip. The engine sounded even and smooth as he turned her around and headed up the channel. I walked up to the bow pulpit and leaned out over the dark, whispering water. I stuck my arms out in front of me, Supergirl-style, and let the wind tear at my face. We rounded the last dock and turned toward the jetty. Jack seemed as adept a⸍ handling the boat as he had been in rebuilding her.

"Let's just keep on going forever!" I shouted over the noise when I made my way back to the cockpit. Jack was standing with the tiller between his legs, steering with his knees.

"Yeah, with about ten gallons of diesel and no mast."

"Come on, Jack. Can't you feel it?" I let out a

war hoop and then threw my arms around his neck. I spoke right into his ear. "*ISLAND HUNTER* wants to go outside, just for a few minutes, Jack."

"No way, not right out of drydock." He shrugged out from my arms and bent down to inspect the oil pressure gauge.

We were halfway out the channel and he started to turn the boat around, to head her back to harbor. I looked at the sea and I told myself to stop, but I couldn't.

"Look, Jack, it's practically flat calm out there. I thought maybe we could just poke her nose out." He wasn't looking at me. "The lei, I thought maybe we could just wet her skirts in the open sea long enough to toss the lei into the water, you know for good luck. Please Jack, I'm not asking to take off to the islands or anything, just to go outside for a couple of minutes. I mean it's no rougher out there than it is in here."

He pushed me down on the seat so hard my head banged into a cockpit winch.

"Stop it!" He tore the lei off and threw it at me, sprinkling the deck with wilted flower petals. "I said no, dammit. A boat can only have one captain."

I rubbed the back of my head and stared at him.

He wouldn't look at me. He kept his eyes straight ahead, focused on the boatyard.

"Look, Tova, I'm sorry, but . . . "

"I didn't wait to hear the rest of it. I walked to

the bow and stood with my feet planted firmly on the deck. I tried to get away, to escape. I hunted for my islands, my dark men, but they were gone. I touched the dolphin at my throat. We'd go on, we'd go out to the Anacapa Inn for our celebration, and I would even order abalone.

I was so cold. I slid up the hood of my sweatshirt and pulled the sleeves down over my hands. I didn't know I was crying until a tear touched my lip and I tasted salt.

Searchin' for the Conch with Uncle Benny

by Mike Lipstock

A revered sailor navigates with
"de visions."

UNCLE BENNY was very slight, with light tan skin and a woolen hat that never left his head. He had never gone to school, but he knew his numbers and behind a tiller could navigate his way to the end of the earth. He could read the color depths of the waters, and at night the stars were his pathways in the sea. He was in his eighties and no one knew where he came from in the Bahamas. Some said Deadman's Reef and others Eight Mile Rock, but it didn't really matter. He just came ashore years ago and never left. Now he was the patriarch of the village and it's unelected leader. He was a master seaman who could skipper anything that sailed, and his other rare ability was . . . magic, insight! He had what the islanders called "de visions." How else was it possible to forecast a catch and track it down in the middle of the ocean? Was it those little flecks of fire that still burned in his eyes? Is that what gave him an extra dimension—an ability to see under water?

Katie and Nick always watched and wondered when they were out to sea with him. The two Americans lived on the same Bahamian island with the old man and cherished him dearly. But he always remained an enigma to them, a mystic who seemed to read their every thought. Off and on they had been coming to the Bahamas for years and now it had finally become home. They had a patched-up old car and a dinky boat with a homemade red sail that they rode the winds with and explored all the islets in their backyard. Most of their friends lived in the hamlets along a shore that went out sixty miles and ended in a small conch village called McCraystown. Out there people still clung to the traditions of 19th-century Britain. There you were addressed as Mister, Mistress, Captain (even if you owned only a rowboat), or, Uncle! the most venerated rank of all. This was reserved for the elders and Uncle Benny was one of the oldest.

Phones didn't exist that far out and only a few could afford electric generators. But they had a

•

Searchin'

for

the

Conch

with

Uncle

Benny

damn long grapevine that spread news over the whole sixty miles of island. For two days now, Katie and Nick were hearing the same story repeatedly. "Dere is big trouble in McCraystown!"

The conch boats had been out for ten days and very few of the conchs had been caught. They needed Uncle Benny to "search dem out" and lead them, but he was off in his boat and couldn't be found. They had their own ideas of bringing him back home, which was based on "de visions" the old man alone possessed. How could you argue with believers of "de mystical powers" when they reasoned like this?

"If de Cap'n and de Mistress come out on de sandy road, Uncle Benny will see dem, dey like his fambly, he'll come rushin' right home!"

The fact that Uncle Benny was on a some small island miles away meant nothing. The answer was "oh, he see dem." Still, it looked as though the Captain and his wife were about to become the "lures."

The very next morning Nick and Kate left with the patched-up car on the most tortuous road in the Bahamas. It was a sandy track just a few feet from the ocean and if the winds blew hard it was washed away. But if it was sunny and calm you rode near gentle waves all foamy and a special color of turquoise, blue, and green. As they drove, Nick said very quietly, "Do you think he can see us coming?" Both wondered silently.

There were reference points to watch for and

after the first fifteen miles the cemetery came into view, the one they planned to rest in for eternity. It was built on an elevation that faced the sea. The small stones rested under the shade of a huge weeping palm. They slowed to a snail's pace and nodded to many old friends who rested there now. Their little Austin mini crunched along the sandy path circling around the water-filled craters that were like small lakes. At thirty miles they came to Pelican's Cove and stopped to talk to the Reverend Mr. Loftus.

"Mornin' Cap'n Nick, Mornin' Mistress Kate."

"Good morning, Reverend," they answered.

"Dey god a lot ob trouble out in McCraystown, de conch has gone away. Dey all waitin' for you to come and bring back Uncle Benny."

"Are you sure he'll come?"

"Cap'n, you and de Mistress are like his fambly, he visions you, when you dere, he'll come."

They knew how vital the conch was to their existence. The meaty mollusk in the big pink shell was their protein source, food staple, and means of making a living. Without it was disaster! Rev. Loftus gave them further news of what to expect a mile or so down the road.

"De sandy road is all washed away to McCraystown. You go to where de casserina tree bends ober de road and follow de 'haul over.' Dis ged you to de beach, de tide is slack, and you god time to drive on de sand all de way."

They thanked him and he shook Nick's hand

•
Searchin'
for
the
Conch
with
Uncle
Benny

and bowed from the waist to Mistress Kate. At the casserina pine they found the path and gingerly drove through the scrub and on to a glorious beach. Not one footstep marred its smooth surface. They threw the mini into high gear on the hard-packed sand and flew; over a splendor that made the eyes smart with joy.

A mile from the end they found a dry piece of road again, and announced their arrival with a toot of the horn. It was a conch town but more like the frontier of the old west—a place where people relied on their own resourcefulness to grow and repair anything.

Now it was almost empty. Only the old and very young remained at home. It was an emergency and everyone was out to sea. The little hamlet was built on a slight rise and the tiny houses all leaned to the side from the buffeting of the winds. Here and there houses were propped with palm trunks but they still managed to outlive their owners. They never collapsed.

Splashes of color were everywhere. A little blue, a dollop of yellow, splotches of orange, and shades of green dabbed on the houses gave the village a feeling of untamed impressionism. Nick and Katie walked into a Monet or Pizzaro painting whenever they arrived. The little car was the only thing that moved. From each door a bent figure shouted out the news.

"Mistress Kate, Cap'n Nick, Uncle Benny come back! He back, he back!" They heard it all the way

Tiller and the Pen

to the end of the quay where they stopped the car and got out. There they found the old man in his tiny house on the edge of the water. The small blue and white house leaned tiredly on a pile of conch shells twenty feet high. No need to honk; he knew they arrived. The smiling old man came out to greet them.

"Aye there Mistress Kate and Cap'n Nick. I knowed since yesterday dat you was comin'."

Katie gave him a big kiss and Nick hugged him by the shoulders. They loved the old man and it was a delight to listen to the lilt of the islands in his speech.

"You knew we were comin'?" Nick asked.

"Oh, I seed you comin' on de sandy road, so I sail in from Little Hog Cay." This had to register with Nick for a moment. 'So the lure did work,' he thought.

"You heard about the conch?"

"Aye, but we find dem. Did you bring de sleepin' bags and some food?" Katie jumped in at this point.

"Uncle Benny, I brought the bags, a case of tuna fish, brown bread, and the ginger ale. We can stay out for a month."

She hit a tender spot when she mentioned the supplies. He loved the tuna, bread, and ginger ale with a passion, and she never forgot.

"Meet me by de boat," he said. "I'll get Uncle Aubert and Rev. Cooper. Dis way we keep dem out ob trouble."

•

Searchin'

for

the

Conch

with

Uncle

Benny

Uncle Aubert and Rev. Cooper were two old conch men his age, who had retired to the backwaters of the docks. They drove to the dock which was just a pile of broken planks and unloaded the small Austin. Katie hadn't forgotten; she brought Aubert and the Reverend big windup clocks. They were overwhelmed with surprise.

Uncle Benny leaned over to Nick and whispered, "Dots some fine gal, huh, Nick!?"

The trip to "somewhere" was about to begin. They walked down to the dock with the supplies. Tied neatly to the crumbling pier was the *Maryanne*, Uncle Benny's sturdy little Abaco sail boat. The Abaco boats were the little hand-hewn ribbed boats made from "de wood from de brush." Each was a work of art, sculpted by primitive hand tools left behind by an ancient ancestor.

A shoal keel; a huge rudder and tiller; and a large sail characterized the Abaco work boat, but the single sail was the distinctive trait. Too poor to buy a good piece of canvas, these were sails of a thousand scraps. They were stitched and patched with pieces of red and blue canvas and some yellow and purple cloth. Ah, but when hoisted, a snootfull of wind swelled the limp rag into a Technicolor marvel.

They loaded the supplies and a big bucket was filled with cold water to cool the ginger ale. Before they left, the Uncles stowed another bucket, this one of live conch—emergency rations they never traveled without. Uncle Aubert and Rev.

Cooper sat in the stern and manned the tiller and sail. Uncle Benny crouched in the bow, and Katie and Nick sat amidships. Nick kept an eye on Uncle Benny to see how he tracked the conch. The sun was dropping and the light was getting dim, but with a crew of masters it made no difference. They headed out to sea and before long the shadow of the island slipped away. It was a long day and Katie and Nick dozed as the little *Maryanne* ploughed through a moonless sea. Sometime in the middle of the night the boat stopped and the five of them came ashore on a desolate island in waters not yet charted.

Nick and Kate, still half asleep, crawled into sleeping bags and the Uncles curled up on the sand in light cotton blankets. At first light they were back in the boat. Uncle Benny led the way with hand signals.

Katie shouted to him, "Do you know where the ships from the village are?"

"Oh yes, Mistress, I know. We be dere in two hours."

And in two hours, just as the clairvoyant predicted, the sixteen wooden Abaco boats stretched out in front of them. Nick and Kate stared at them in wonder. Never before had they seen the whole fleet sailing in full regalia. What a sight! Most of the hulls were white with a little green and red trim, but oh, those sails! The patched colors were in stripes, diagonals, circles and hundreds of geometric designs. Wind filled, they

•

Searchin'

for

the

Conch

with

Uncle

Benny

headed directly to the *Maryanne*. It was an astonishing sight, a moment in time that Nick and Kate would never forget.

The Uncles would lead in "de search for de conch" and the fleet would follow. Uncle Benny's hand signals and built-in radar were going to find an elusive herd of conch somewhere in the middle of the ocean.

The old man sat in the bow, eyes squinting in the sun. They headed further east into much deeper water. Was he on to something? Islanders rarely left the safety of the reef and that they did awhile ago. In deep water everything changed color. They were sailing in an ocean of royal blue and only in the shallows where the conch lived would it turn back to turquoise.

Meanwhile Nick marveled at the old man who was following a preordained course from which he never wavered. His hand worked like an extra rudder—every eye was on it. A slight wave to port and the fleet adjusted immediately. Their confidence was back. Most probably recalled from long ago, when the old man had taken them far away to the Caico's and they returned with a full bounty of conch.

As they cut across the open sea, Nick could dimly make out the outline of a distant landfall. An island began emerging, one not on the charts. The color of the water was turning to a familiar light green and the island now stood in sharp relief. Suddenly the old man stood up in the bow and raised his hand to round up and stop. The clan followed with great emotion. Had he found the conch? Uncle Aubert dropped the sail and Rev. Cooper prayed. Uncle Benny though, had "de big grin on his face!"

"Dose boys, he said, miss de whole conch march. Dey was sailin' de wrong way. Dey right under de boat. Can't you see dem, Mistress?"

They squinted into the water and saw what appeared to be rocks. With a sudden roar the water churned white as the villagers stooped to pick up the mother lode found by the great Uncle Benny. Katie and Nick joined the harvest and loaded conch until their arms were numb. In the evening with the ships loaded to the gunwales, the five of them waded ashore and settled in for another night under the stars.

Nick was looking for answers. The whole trip was a puzzle to him.

"What made you go to that island for the conch, Uncle?"

"I had de visions."

"You could see across miles and miles of open ocean?"

"I could see de little marks dey make in de sand, and dots what I follow."

"When did you know there were so many out there?"

"I look under de water and dere are de feelers stickin' out ob de sand. De furder we go, de more dey come up."

•

Searchin'

for

the

Conch

with

Uncle

Benny

"Did you see them in the deep water also?"

"Oh yes, dots when I seed dem best."

That's where the conversation ended. Nick shook his head and went to help Katie who was busy making a ton of tuna salad that the Uncles loved with their brown bread and ginger ale. There were no answers for Uncle Benny's magic, it just happened. Nick had to leave it in the same niche as UFO's and sci-fi tales.

It had been a wonderful adventure and that night secure in their bedrolls, Nick and Kate's hands crept out and entwined in secret embrace.

La Corona del Diablo

by Ray Bradley

*An eighteenth-century Spanish
mariner encounters a mystical
crown of fabulous beauty and
spellbinding power.*

WAVE AFTER WAVE crashed over the bow of the Spanish galleon, each mountain of water hammering the ship with a force that threatened to separate her frame from her keel. Oaken timbers, wrenched by the blows, groaned in protest. After every impact, she shuddered and, like an injured animal, shook herself and gathered her strength to spring upon the next wave racing toward her. Every time she clawed her way up the incline of the rising sea, her bowsprit

penetrated the towering wall of water, appearing
to release it to thunder down upon her deck and
return to the sea in green grey torrents through her
gun ports and scuppers.

The wind tore at the man of war's reefed sails,
ripping stitching and shredding panels, leaving
only tattered streamers of fabric. Only the main
mast, the stoutest, remained. The other two,
snapped like match sticks by the force of the wind,
trailed in the sea or lay on the deck in a tangle of
rigging, canvas, and splintered spruce. Buffeted
and deafened by the wind, several crew members
struggled ineffectively to clear the wreckage from
the pitching and rolling deck. They worked with
one hand while gripping the rail or rigging with the
other, stopping to grasp a hold with both hands
every time the sea washed over them. An excep-
tionally large wave engulfed them, and one sailor,
unable to hold on, was swept before it over the rail
into the raging water below. His scream, a futile
cry swallowed by the howling wind, never reached
his shipmates.

Two men clung to the ship's wheel, strug-
gling to keep the vessel from broaching. One,
Hernando Mendoza de Castilla, was the captain.
Less than three weeks earlier, on February 3, 1738,
Mendoza had sailed his command, the warship *La
Victoria*, along with five other vessels from Veracruz.
Aboard was a consignment of gold and silver,
Registry treasure, to be transported to Spain for the
coffers of King Phillip V. It was the *norte* season,

and Mendoza had hoped for a fast passage, allowing the fleet from *Nueva España* to clear the Caribbean without encountering a storm. But winds were light and their progress slow. It had taken them ten days just to reach Havana where they rendezvoused with four more ships from Cartageña, the *Tierra Firme* flota. These ships would join them for the journey across the Atlantic to Spain.

While anchored at Havana, taking on provisions for the long passage home, Mendoza saw for the first time La Corona del Diablo, the Devil's Crown. As was the custom, port officials boarded the vessel to inspect the treasure, a precaution taken to discourage pilferage during the voyage from Mexico.

Although regulations mandated the ship's captain be present during the procedure, Mendoza's involvement had been, at most, that of a disinterested spectator. He stood by idly while the King's men inventoried each chest and crate, checking the contents against the manifest prepared in Veracruz. He did not covet the ingots of silver and sacks of gold coins. Not that he shunned wealth, but three earlier trips to the New World, from which he returned to Spain laden with treasure, had made him a rich man. He wasn't about to risk death on the gallows to increase his fortune with a portion of the King's riches.

But when a small, highly polished mahogany chest was lifted from its storage place and opened, his interest awakened. Inside, resting in a nest of black satin, was the most beautiful object he had ever seen. There lay a crown intricately fashioned from three alloys of gold, each exhibiting its own rich hue of orange and yellow. The ornately filigreed band of metals was adorned with amethyst, emerald, and garnet stones. A series of gold spikes, each topped with a large turquoise, crested the jeweled base. In the dim cargo hold the lantern light reflected from the gem facets and carved gold surfaces and stole Mendoza's breath. There and then he decided the crown must be his.

Later, during the night, he returned to the hold and, using a key only he possessed, opened the door to the treasure vault and removed the mahogany chest containing the crown. Clutching it under his arm, he returned to his cabin where he hid it beneath his bunk. He remained awake the entire night, sitting at his desk, repeatedly removing his treasure to admire its beauty and run his finger tips across its delicate surfaces. It was his. He commanded its beauty. He cared not for the consequences of his thievery. He had become bedeviled, the victim of its exquisiteness, captured by the spell of La Corona del Diablo.

Four days later, the small fleet, four galleons and six naos, set sail from Havana. A route had been planned that would carry them north, passing to the east of *Los Martires,* the Florida Keys, and to the west of the Bahamas. However, after barely clearing the harbor, the wind strengthened and, strangely, swung around from the north. Sailing their original course became impossible. So the treasure-laden convoy fell off onto an easterly heading to skirt Cuba's northern coast just beyond the grasp of its shoreline reefs.

Over the next few days the brisk winds continued, forcing the fleet to maintain a course that followed the Lesser Antilles chain of islands. Mesmerized by his newly acquired possession, Mendoza failed to consider navigating the convoy along a safer alternate course. His thoughts were occupied with what ownership of the crown would mean when he returned to Castile. He envisioned the wonderment of his friends and delighted in the anticipation of their envy. He became enraptured . . . and the fleet sailed on.

Then, while still in sight of Puerto Rico, the wind increased and the seas started to build. Mendoza consulted the other captains. Trusting that the freshening air was nothing more than that, they bypassed San Juan hoping to benefit from a faster passage enabled by the stronger wind.

It was a fateful decision. No sooner had San Juan been passed then conditions started to worsen. Within a few hours the storm tore into the flotilla, assailing the ships with gale force winds and twenty-foot seas. Disoriented and unable to see the other ships, Mendoza and his crew sailed on blindly, hoping for the best. After shortening sail they made headway for awhile, but the force of the wind was too much. The vessel began to break up. Control was lost.

The crew worked desperately just to keep the galleon afloat and off the hundreds of reefs and shoals strewn throughout the Leeward Islands. With each onslaught by the sea, Mendoza and the helmsman strained at the wheel to keep the disintegrating ship headed into the waves. They had no idea of their location. Visibility was limited to fleeting glimpses of a dark sky alternately eclipsed by the onrushing waves of an angry sea. Each time the ship plunged off the back side of a wave, Mendoza braced himself in anticipation of the shuddering crash that would signal *La Victoria's* death on some hidden coral reef. The exhilaration he felt in contemplating the pleasure La Corona del Diablo would give him faded. He even offered the crown in sacrifice to whatever gods were besieging him. Finally, in desperation, he alternated praying to the Virgin Mother and the devil for deliverance. Neither heard him.

The expected occurred at a moment when Mendoza thought his prayers might have been answered. To their left, a small break in the scurrying clouds, a light in the blackness, rallied his hope. He yelled into the helmsman's ear and excitedly pointed to his discovery. Below them, the ship struggled up yet another wave and careened down the other side. Mendoza tightened his grip, refocused forward, and waited to see which way they'd veer at the bottom. What he saw caused his heart to race and brought the cold chill of eminent death to his being. Before the bow was land! It appeared ominous and dark against the nearly black sea, made visible only by the frothing water around the submerged reefs.

Instinctively he strained to turn the wheel to starboard. The ship responded sluggishly, barely turning before the next wave struck. The impact turned them broadside to the seas, and instead of climbing the face of the next wave, the galleon rolled on her side. The tattered sail filled with water, snapping the one remaining mast just above the deck and dragging it into the sea along with the on-deck crew. Mendoza fell across the deck, his last thought being of La Corona del Diablo, his last awareness being of the ship's rail looming below him and the black water beneath it. His body crashed into the rail, crushing his chest and breaking his back. Mercifully unconscious, he toppled over the rail and dropped into the sea.

Another wave lifted *La Victoria* and then rolled out from beneath the mortally wounded ship, allowing it to right itself as it slid helplessly into the following trough. Again it rose and again it fell, wallowing and rolling, until it washed onto the shoals of Anegada Island. On the first impact the hull was impaled on a reef, several coral heads ripped through the thin lead sheeting, cracking and splitting the planking. Again and again the sea lifted its victim, dashing it repeatedly against the coral. Its keel broken and its ribs shattered, *La Victoria* began to settle below the waves.

The gold and silver she carried spilled from her cargo hold, settling in the bilge among the iron ingots that had been her ballast. For a few minutes, the high stern of the galleon, the captain's quarters, remained above the angry waters. Then slowly, as though tired by its ordeal, it rolled over and, succumbing to the battering of the surf, disintegrated. A small mahogany chest drifted down through the water along with the debris and settled amidst the silver and iron bars and sacks of gold.

Over the years, while the action of the waves and the passing of time completed the destruction started by the storm, the treasure would sift through the broken hull onto the floor of the sea. There it would lay to be covered by the shifting sands and the sediment of the decaying wreck, there to rest until rediscovered by some future mariner, freeing La Corona del Diablo to once again cast its spell.

About the Contributors

—In order of appearance —

John Ellsworth *—Editor*

John Ellsworth, who holds a master's license and a doctorate, is an associate professor of communication at Nassau Community College on Long Island, NY. His work has appeared in *Sail, Boating, Small Boat Journal,* and *Our Navy* magazines, as well as in the books *The Best of Sail Navigation* (Sail Books, 1982) and *The North University Cruising Course* (North Sails, 1990). He has also reviewed books for *The New York Times,* McGraw-Hill, and Harcourt Brace.

A former quartermaster for the U.S. Navy, Ellsworth worked during the 1970s as an editor for Pan American Airways, a delivery skipper, and a sailing instructor. For three summers in the early 1980s, he also taught sailing as an island skipper for Sail Caribbean Voyages.

Barry Rockwell —*Illustrator*

Before turning to full-time freelancing, Barry Rockwell illustrated comic books and was an art director for several advertising agencies. His work has appeared in the ads of Mobil Oil, UniRoyal Tires, Long Island Railroad, and many others. He has also illustrated for *Newsday* and rendered jacket art for Doubleday Books. He is known for his humorous American portraits, several of which have won awards.

The Long Island Convention and Visitors Bureau recently commissioned Rockwell to create a large painting to be the official showpiece of the 1994 Long Island Fall Festival. The painting was published as a poster in a limited edition of 2000.

Rockwell has been sailing all his life. Among his ventures are eight or nine charters in the West Indies.

John Tucker *Cutting Rope*

John Tucker is a teacher, writer, and musician. "Cutting Rope" is based on experiences while crewing on a down-east windjammer in his teens. Tucker teaches writing and literature at Nassau Community College and Columbia University. His most recent project was co-composing and co-music directing for *Lightin' Out: The Mark Twain Musical*, an Off-Broadway show based on Twain's life and works.

Eton Churchill *Three Men and a Boat*

Churchill is a professor of communications at Penn State. He is a native of Maine where he returns by sail each summer aboard his 12-year old wooden ketch, *Glad Tidings*.

Churchill has produced several sea films, the most notable being *Home to the Sea* (for PBS) about Maine's maritime heritage. To his credit is a children's book about the Maine islands, *Mind How the Sun Goes* (1974). Several years ago, he made a sabbatical sojourn to Grenada. Parts of the trip were chronicled in *Cruising World* under the title "Mal de Port." Churchill also reviews videos for *WoodenBoat* and writes screen plays and corporate scripts.

At Penn State he focuses on contemporary rhetoric and its influence on the formation of the self. He has several publications in this area as well.

Marian Blue *Standing Watch*

Marian Blue, a freelance writer for seventeen years, has published fiction, poetry, essays, and journalism. Her work has appeared in a variety of publications including *Chesapeake Bay Magazine*, *Coastal Cruising*, *Cruising World*, *Sail*, and *Soundings*. Her article in *Portfolio Magazine*, "Duel in the Wind—Racing vs. Cruising Sailors," received a Virginia Press Award in 1990 as a first place in sports writing. Marian is currently living in a cabin in the Pacific Northwest, writing full-time.

Tiller and the Pen

Ben Wilensky *Coffee on the Watch*

Over forty years ago Wilensky shipped foreign, union, and non-union as a wiper and ordinary seaman. A collection of his sea poetry, *The Psalms of a Sailor Jew*, will be published in 1994-95 by the Edwin Mellen Press.

Joan Connor *Aground*

Joan Connor has published over forty short stories in various anthologies and journals, among them *Blueline*, *The Worcester Review*, Re: *Artes Liberales*, and *The Bridge*. "Aground" was a finalist for the 1992 Writers' Voice Award and first appeared in *The North American Review*. She is currently working on her first novel begun on a fellowship at MacDowell and is an M.F.A. candidate at Vermont College.

Gregory Fitz Gerald *The Sea has many Voices*

Fitz Gerald, who earned a Ph.D. from the University of Iowa, is a professor at the State University of New York (SUNY)—Brockport, where he teaches fiction writing.

His books include *Hunting the Yahoos; Modern Satiric Stories: The Impropriety Principle; Neutron Stars; The Late, Great Future* (with John Dillon); *Past, Present, and Future Perfect* (with Jack Wolf); *The Druze Document* (also with John Dillon); and *The Hidden Quantum*.

Fitz Gerald's short fiction, essays, and poetry

have appeared in widely diverse periodicals and anthologies in the United States, Canada, England, Ireland, Australia, and New Zealand.

At SUNY, Fitz Gerald founded the Brockport *Writer's Forum*—an internationally known series of literary readings, writing workshops, lectures, and television interviews. He has served twice as its director.

Daniel Spurr *Wreck of the Juniper*

Daniel Spurr, of Newport, Rhode Island, is the editor of *Practical Sailor* magazine. He holds an M.A. in English from Johns Hopkins University. He was senior editor of *Cruising World* magazine until 1987 when he and his wife Andra cruised their sailboat from Newport to the Canadian border, then south to Key West and the Bahamas.

Spurr has two living children, Adriana, twenty-three, and Stephen, six, both whom acquired their father's love of the sea—sailing, fishing, and messing about in boats. At last count there were four in various states of disrepair: a Tartan 44, a 16-foot three-part rowing skiff, a pram dinghy, and an antique wooden Sunfish with a terminal case of dry rot.

Spurr is the author of three books, *Spurr's Boatbook: Upgrading the Cruising Sailboat*, 1983, 2nd edition, 1991; *Yacht Style*, 1990; and *Steered by the Falling Stars: A Father's Journey*, 1992.

Michael Badham   *Flo*

Since retiring in 1960 as a submarine captain in the Royal Navy, Michael Badham has spent much time writing and chartering boats he's either refit or built. He first ocean-proofed a 57-year old 43-foot R.N.L.I. lifeboat and sailed the Atlantic with his family—including two- and four-year-old children. After chartering the vessel in Antigua, he returned to England and built a 45-foot Piver trimaran. He then resumed chartering in the Caribbean. Eventually he sailed north to charter with the New York Yacht Club's annual cruise and to view the America's Cup.

Later with another wife, he settled down in Ireland to build ferro-cement houseboats to charter on the River Shannon. They stayed eight years before moving to Maine. He's now trying to eke out a living writing. Badham has written for *Nautical Quarterly, Offshore, Small Boat Journal,* and many other periodicals.

Mary Lee Coe   *Foggy Foggy Don'ts*

Mary Lee Coe has stories in *Other Voices, The Louisville Review,* and *Kansas Quarterly,* and essays in *Bloomsbury Review* and *New Letters Review of Books.* She teaches writing at the University of Southern Maine, in Portland, where her husband is a sailmaker.

Richard Morris Dey   *A Daughter of the Tradewind*

Richard Dey, once a commercial fisherman and schooner skipper, is now a book editor and a freelance journalist. A former poetry editor of the *Harvard Advocate*, he has published work in *Sail* and *Poetry* magazines, as well as several others. *The Loss of the Schooner "Kestrel,"* a collection of his poems related to the sea, is due out from James Cummins, late in 1994. He also has published in chapbook form an extended essay-interview, *In the Way of Adventure: John Caldwell and Palm Island.* "A Daughter of the Tradewind" originally appeared in his book, *The Bequia Poems*, published by Macmillan Caribbean.

Tamsen Merrill   *The Cruise of the Diablesse*

Tamsen Merrill spent her earlier summers racing plywood Turnabouts in the harbor at Nantucket Island. Family adventures included extended cruises in Maine and among the islands of Denmark.

Ms. Merrill attended Bennington College where she majored in creative writing. She worked in France, received a degree in French literature from a French university, dabbled in public television work, and was editor of her small-town monthly newspaper in western Massachusetts. She still lives in that town with her husband and two children, writing all the while.

Christine Kling   *Island Hunter*

Christine Kling has been a freelance writer for many of her cruising years. Her articles have appeared in *MotorBoating & Sailing*, *Sailing*, and *Los Angeles Magazine*. Recently she turned to fiction writing, and earned an M.F.A. in creative writing at Florida International University. Her first published short story appeared in the literary magazine, *Gulf Stream*. Another short story, "Flight," received second place in the Porter Flemming Writing competition judged by Robert Olen Butler.

In 1993 she took a two-year leave of absence from teaching creative writing at a Miami high school to cruise with her husband aboard their 55-foot cutter, *SUNRISE*. In the winter of 1994 they were in St. Martin, eventually headed for Venezuela and Trinidad for the hurricane season. *SUNRISE* should be "home" by the spring of 1995, after which Christine plans to look for a university position.

Mike Lipstock   *Searchin' for de Conch with Uncle Benny*

Mike Lipstock is a 71-year-old who took up writing four years ago. His short stories have appeared in over sixty magazines and anthologies and he has recently completed a screen play. He lives in Jericho, New York with his wife of fifty years.

Ray Bradley *La Corona del Diablo*

At age fifty-five, Ray Bradley retired from an executive position in industry and began writing, fulfilling a desire suppressed throughout his professional career. In writing "La Corona del Diablo," he drew upon ten years of sailing experience in one-design boats and offshore cruisers.

He recently sold publishing rights to his first novel, *Cadence Count,* a "cozy mystery." He is seeking a publisher for a second novel, *Chasing the Dragon,* and is nearing completion of a third, a sailing adventure set in the Caribbean.

Glossary

For readers less familiar with the jargon of sail . . .

---

abeam *Said of anything abreast a vessel.*

astern 41 *Said of anything behind a vessel.*

batten 114 *One of several flexible strips of wood or synthetic material placed in slots at the trailing edge of a sail (leech) to keep it flat.*

Beaufort Wind Scale *An international scale for measuring wind velocity. Stronger winds have higher numbers, which range from 0-17. For example: Force 4 is a moderate breeze at 11-16 knots with small waves. Force 5 is a fresh breeze at 17-21 knots with moderate waves. Force 9 is a strong gale at 41-47 knots with high waves and dense foam. Forces 12-17 are hurricane winds of 64 knots and above. Waves? You can imagine!*

beat, to 14 *To sail toward the wind in a zigzag course. Also see* tack.

before the wind 113 *To sail with the wind.   Also see* off the wind *and* wing-and-wing.

bend, to 61 *To fasten a sail to a stay.*

brigantine ix *A two-masted vessel having square-rigged sails forward and a fore-and-aft sail aft with square topsails aloft.*

broaching (to) 158   *When a vessel veers broadside to the wind and waves. Such a vessel may be in danger and out of control.*

broad reach 113   *See* reach.

close hauled 113   *Sailing nearly into the wind, or "on the wind." The sails will be hauled close to the centerline of the boat.*

cutter 125, 172   *A vessel which carries two headsails, a jib set on the headstay, which runs to the stem, and a staysail set on an inner forestay which runs to the foredeck. Also see* stay.

dead reckoning 62   *To navigate by compass and log (time and distance) while compensating for current and wind force and direction.*

fairlead 61   *A ring or block through which rigging runs easily without snagging or chafing.*

Force 4, 5, 9 72, 73, 75   *See* Beaufort Wind Scale.

forestay 64, 78   *See* stay.

gaff 41, 94, 115   *A spar attached to a mast on which the upper edge of a sail is extended; thus a sail or vessel may be gaff-headed or gaff-rigged.*

glass 73, 74   *Nautical slang for barometer.*

gunwale (gunnel) 54, 114   *A railing around a vessel.*

halyard 4   *Line or cable (running rigging) used to hoist and lower a sail.*

hank 61, 78   *A shackle, most often in a series along the luff (leading edge) of a jib used to fasten the sail to the forestay. "To hank" is to fasten using hanks.*

hard over (hard alee) 15   *A command to push the tiller all the way to the lee side of the vessel when coming about (changing tack).*

hard to windward 93   *Optimally sailing close hauled, right on the wind.*

headed up 37   *When a vessel is facing the wind.*

hove-to (heave to) 74, 78   *To hold a sailing vessel into the wind and remain motionless except for drifting. Usually done to weather a storm.*

in irons 64   *When a vessel stops during a tack with the wind dead ahead and cannot be turned either way.*

jib 14–15, 19, 20   *A triangular headsail flown off the headstay.*

ketch 100, 117   *A sailing vessel with two masts, the mainmast stepped forward, the shorter mizzenmast stepped aft, forward of the rudder post. Also see* yawl.

lapstrake 77   *A type of small-craft construction characterized by overlapping planks.*

lee *or* **leeward** 93, 116, 118   *The side away from the wind.*

mizzen 13, 73   *The stern sail on a ketch or yawl, set on the mizzenmast.*

nao 160   *An early Spanish ocean-sailing vessel somewhat smaller than a galleon.*

off the wind 13, 116   *Sailing before the wind.*

on the wind   *See* close hauled.

painter 52   *A line used to tow or secure a small boat or dinghy.*

pointing 117   *Sailing close to the wind.*

points of sail   *Various sailboat positions relative to the wind: close hauled (on the wind), reaching (wind abeam, or thereabouts), and running (off the wind).*

reach 16   *A point of sail with three variations: When the wind is abeam, a boat is sailing on a* beam *reach. When the wind is coming from behind but not directly astern (abaft the beam or on the quarter), the boat is on a* broad *reach. When the wind is forward of the beam, but not close-hauled, the boat is sailing on a* close *reach.*

ready about 15 *A command that alerts crew to standby to change tack. The command is followed by "hard alee" or "hard over."*

reef, to 41, 73 *To reduce the sail area by rolling or folding the lower part and securing it with short line called reef points.*

reeve, to 61 *To thread a line through a block (pulley) or fairlead.*

R.N.L.I. 70, 170 *The Royal National Lifeboat Institute, the organization responsible for coastal sea rescue in Great Britain.*

schooner 5–7, 92, 93 *A sailing vessel with two or more masts, a foremast, and a mainmast stepped nearly amidships.*

sheets 15, 21, 61 *Lines (running rigging) used to adjust a sail's angle to the wind. One eases (lets out) or trims (hauls in) the sheets.*

shoot the sun, to 75 *To aim a sextant at the sun (take a sighting) to obtain a sunline, a function of celestial navigation.*

shorten sail, to 41 *To reduce the sail area by reefing. Necessary when winds are excessive.*

sloop 19, 20, 21, 57, 77 *A one-masted boat rigged with a jib and a mainsail.*

spinnaker 97 *A light, relatively large triangular sail flown over the bow when sailing downwind.*

spitfire jib 73 *A very small jib made of strong material flown in rough weather. Also referred to as a storm jib.*

stay 93 *A line or cable, as part of standing rigging, that supports a mast (e.g., headstay, forestay, backstay). Headsails are set on most forward stays. Also see cutter.*

steadying sail 31 *A small sail set on a fishing or cruising trawler, used to reduce rolling in a broadside sea.*

steerageway vi *When a vessel has sufficient motion to respond to its rudder.*

tack *or* **tacking, to** 6, 14–17, 93, 113, 114, 125 *The process of bringing a vessel's head through the wind to get the wind on the other side. Necessary when sailing toward the wind (upwind); results in sailing a zigzag course.*

telltale 64 *A short string or cloth tied to the rigging that indicates wind direction.*

trysail 41 *A fore-and-aft, gaffed-rigged sail set aft on some two-masted square riggers such as men-of-war brigs.*
    On a smaller offshore sailing vessel, the trysail is a strong triangular sail flown during heavy weather.

upwind *Toward the wind.*

winch 14, 15 *A drum around which a line is coiled and cranked to make it easier to pull that line. Commonly used to trim sheets or hoist a sail.*

wing-and-wing 95 *When sails are on both sides of a boat sailing downwind.*

yawl *A sailing vessel with two masts, the mainmast stepped forward, the shorter mizzenmast stepped* <u>abaft</u> *(behind) the rudder post. Also see* ketch.